THERE WILL BE WAR

THERE WILL BE WAR

THE PUPPET MASTER SAGA

SIDHARTH KHER

PARTRIDGE

A Penguin Random House Company

To order additional copies of this book, contact
Partridge India
000 800 10062 62
www.partridgepublishing.com/india
orders.india@partridgepublishing.com

To J.R.R Tolkien, Christopher Paolini, Eoin Colfer, Rick Riordan, Hiro Mashima and Tite Kubo for the inspiration of a lifetime. And to my father, the one who made this possible.

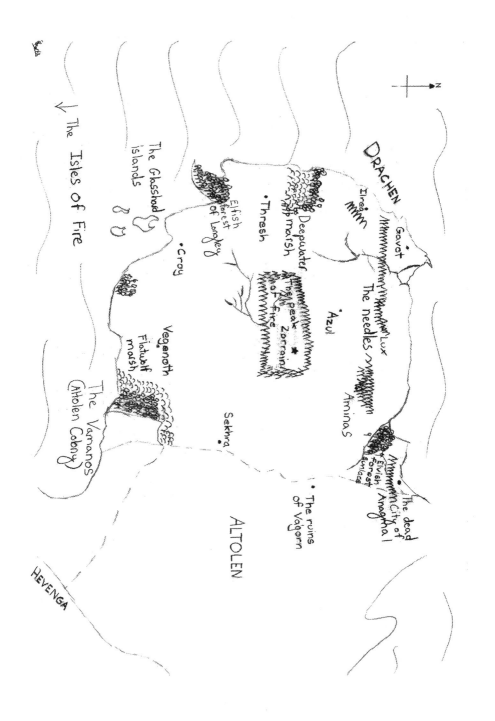

The Warring Lands

Harpe
Allbay
Goban
Horsh

Jotun's Fall

The Frostclaws

The Crack
of the Abyss

The Cisternlands

The Ilses
of
Fire

The Dragons'
Teeth

The Southern
Marshes

South Hevenga
(Mostly
Deserted)

N

CONTENTS

A BRIEF EXPLANATION OF THE PUPPET MASTER UNIVERSE

Yeah hi, this is the author speaking, yes Sidharth Kher, this is the explanatory part of the book that acts like a reference if you have any queries while reading the Puppet Master [for convenience I am going to start calling The Puppet Master Universe: PMU]. These few pages are here to help you with the slightly confusing bits like Gods and Magic and NOT the plot.

The story unfolds in a time period similar to 900-985 Europe, a time full of chivalrous knights, powerful and greedy kings and suffering peasants.

In the PMU there are creatures call knaves. [It is pronounced knaa-veys] There is an organization called the Facce Pax [Pronounced: fachay pax], they ride the Knaves, they were the general peace keepers of the universe, Facce Pax are selected from people who have a high magical capacity so that it doesn't take years for them to learn the most basic magics.

Oh yeah, I forgot to add, in this universe the story takes place on one continent. It is divided into three major empires Drachen, Altolen and Hevenga. Altolen is the opposite of Drachen, that is, it full of people who have integrity and has only a small amount of criminals.

Moving on . . . in the beginning you'll read about something called the Great Evil. Let's get one thing straight, they are a vast horde of monsters and soldiers who are, well, evil who have banded together for the greater [oh this sounds so wrong] evil. They ARE NOT, some evil guys syndicate.

There are gods in the PMU and people have communicated with them and seen them. In Norse mythology the gods are divided into two groups; Aesir and Vanir. Well in the PMU it is like that also, except unlike the Aesir and Vanir the two groups of gods hate each other and would willingly fight to the death with each other, if there was a death for them.

Another thing, Elf and Demon magic aren't the only form of magic in the PMU, they are just some of the useful spells that the initial Facce Pax liked a bit more than the rest and thought that they would come in handy for future generations.

Not all people are capable of magic, but each one who is, has his own personal ability, from changing to color of other peoples fingernail, and making small things catch fire to being able to detonate ICBM[1] size explosions with the mind.

Another thing about gods, Demipowers are mini gods, there not important enough to become gods, but they're immortal beings that exist up there with the gods.[2]

---

[1] An ICBM is an intercontinental ballistic missile [a big bang-bang thing that big countries use to threaten little countries with.] and **IS NOT** in the Puppet master at any point of time

[2] They are like the angel's of Christianity, not as powerful as God but immortal nevertheless

PROLOGUE

THE FACCE PAX OF TANIS

PART ONE
THE DOOMKNIGHTS

First there were only Knaves, and they roamed the land in harmony. Then came the elves. The two species instantly became rivals and warred for many years. Then entered the Dwarves, from their caves, they too joined this war. The war continued for a decade and ravaged each race.

So a truce was called and a corps was established to keep the peace: The Facce Pax. A Knaves and a rider would work hand in hand to keep the peace.

However a problem arose. Who would ride the Knaves? Amidst this problem the human race arrived in ships from the south. They agreed to ride the Knaves and would function as peacekeepers.

Four thousand years passed and then disaster struck; the formerly weak and restricted evils had seen the Facce Pax slowly losing their edge. Their high council was corrupt and lazy. To top it off they refused to see the power of the evil that was at their gates.

The Great Evil easily swept through the lands crushing all in their path, whether it was a standard raised by a Vicar, or a legion of a King's finest men they left nothing behind except burned fields and innumerable corpses. Kings from all across the continent appealed to the High Council of the Facce Pax in vain.

At last when the continent was almost completely in the clutches of Great Evil the council finally declared war, the great army of the Facce Pax stood up to fight against the Great Evil.

But after the first few skirmishes it became apparent that the army of the Facce Pax was not what it used to be. In the beginning the Facce Pax and their allies almost always had the advantage of numbers, but each and every time they were humiliatingly routed.

*   *   *

"ARCHERS, TAKE AIM!" The order broke through the silence of the evening. The Facce Pax had amassed a host of thirty thousand men, and the Great Evil had responded by sending twenty five thousand soldiers.

The two armies were three hundred feet away from each other. Xephos Seize, the commander of the Great Evil's forces strode behind the line of archers. He turned to his lieutenant. "Fire when deemed fit." With that he walked back to his tent.

The Facce Pax made their move.

Knaves and their riders flew overhead, lines of soldiers advanced. "ARCHERS READY!" shouted the lieutenant. The first few lines of the Facce Pax forces broke into a run. "FIRE ALL!" the lieutenant screamed.

The lieutenant drew his sword and charged to meet the enemy. Shields clashed, swords clanged and the battlefield echoed with the screams of soldiers.

The Facce Pax pushed hard. The battle had high stakes and the winner would secure a foothold for a new campaign. The Great Evil was hit hard on all fronts. Within the first twenty minutes, the Great Evil sustained almost two and a half thousand casualties.

The Facce Pax's troops cut a swath through their enemies. The battered Great Evil was on its knees. Then Xephos Seize came out of his tent.

The commander radiated power; his very presence seemed to empower the soldiers on the front line. Seize surveyed the battlefield. He frowned. Xephos Seize did not like losing. So he drew his blade. And so the storm of Xephos Seize began.

What happened then, no one could explain. The Facce Pax was utterly annihilated. Less than a thousand soldiers left the battlefield alive. The few members of the Facce Pax who got out were scarred and bloody.

By now the Facce Pax knew they could not win. Any chance of a counter attack was gone. However no one would have guessed what would occur next.

*   *   *

"Xephos Seize," It was in the Headquarters of the Great Evil, a man stood up and exclaimed, "What an honor it is to finally meet the prodigy who has the great generals of our army gossiping."

He was wearing a fine black cloak with a silver trim; the black wreath on his head showing his high rank the man himself in question was tall and well built with innumerable scars on his face. "My name is Orisis Kazekage, and I have a business proposal for you . . ."

Seize wore a red cloak, a black cape and a Spartan like helmet he was also freakishly tall at six feet seven inches. "I want you to meet a couple friends of mine." Orisis said as they walked down a corridor.

Orisis suddenly stopped, startling Seize. "Through this door," he said turning, he opened it. Seated inside there were eight men, most of whom he knew. "Welcome Lord Seize to the Doomknights . . ."

In the next three weeks, people saw things that they never thought they would see. For three weeks the armies of evil stood still, not a soldier was sent to scout or attack. Rumors started spreading that the Great Evil was facing political infighting, those rumors were correct.

Then the Great Evil struck so hard and so fast that not many people were sure what happened. All that people knew was that the Great Evil had finally wiped nearly all of the Facce Pax out. They mercilessly razed all remaining resistance, they controlled the all of the continent that was not in the hands of their two other rival empires, Altelon and Hevenga.

At the public celebration Orisis Kazekage arrived and gave a speech. Most people thought that it was something to put Orisis in the people's favor. But the wise ones knew what was really going, Orisis had assumed the title of Lord and he was now in control, he was now King and was assisted by his lieutenants; the Doomknights.

The empire of the Great Evil had died, and from its ashes rose a nation far more powerful and united: Drachen.

*   *   *

"Doomknights," came the hard voice of Orisis. There were five people in the room, each more valuable than a battalion of soldiers. Upon hearing Orisis' voice they all snapped to attention. "The others are currently deployed; they are consolidating our boundaries with Altolen. There is no need to wait."

"Down with Altolen." One of the men spat. It was Ishvala Negundo, an alchemist, his extraordinary manipulation of the elements left a great impression on Orisis.

"If I may ask, my liege, where are we?" asked Xephos Seize. The question itself was a good one. Orisis himself didn't know the whole answer. They were in a cave under the southern city of Vegenath. The cave itself ordinary, grey stone, several stalagmites and various other features one finds in caves.

Orisis believed that it was used as a secret storage, being located under the house of a wealthy merchant. He however did not look into the cave too deeply. He had people who would do that later.

"That is of no relevance." Orisis said. Seize bowed his head in acknowledgement.

"However, I would not have summoned all of you here if I did not have something relevant to say." All five Doomknights looked at him intently. "One of your own has left us forever."

The Doomknights immediately stood up straight. It was serious. Orisis continued. "The Sixth Doomknight has deserted. He prefers to consort with the rebelling fools."

Each Doomknight knew what this meant. Any association with the rebels was punishable by death. "When did this happen?" someone asked. The voice belonged to Sir Edmund Shadoe, a brilliant necromancer. It was said that he personally created an army of ten thousand undead to serve Orisis.

"Two weeks ago, *Lord* Shadoe. I am confident, though, that he did not manage to leak any high risk information." Orisis said. Despite the fact that Shadoe was rightfully a Lord, he preferred his 'sir' title. This annoyed Orisis a good deal. He stressed on the title of 'lord' whenever he could.

"He will most likely try to join the few members of the Facce Pax that remain. I am confident, that you will be able to find him." Orisis said menacingly. This was not a statement; it was a direct order.

"I will make it my top priority my liege." Came the voice of Shrukin Fiefdom, despite his thin and sickly appearance, he was a Doomknight for a reason. Shrukin was perhaps the greatest tactician, political counselor and general advisor in existence.

"We will spring a trap to lure him out, and then we will bring him before you." Shrukin continued. "As much as I admire your enthusiasm Shrukin," Orisis remarked "six will be expecting something like this. You must do something radically different."

Shrukin bowed. "It will be done my liege." Orisis was content. The Doomknights knew what they had to do. "Excellent. Leave now, all of you, you have your orders." The five walked towards the mouth of the cave. The fifth one, however Orisis stopped. "You do not deceive me Katsura, I am not a fool."

Orisis grabbed Katsura by the collar and flung him to the ground. "Lord Hyorin Katsura, you maybe half demon, but don't not think that you can outsmart me." Hyorin Katsura got up. "Forgive me my liege." His voice was devoid of guilt or fear.

"I know very well that you have been stealing runes from me. I swear to Hell and all things in it, if you think you can hide something from me you are mistaken." "Again, I apologize, my liege." Katsura said slyly.

"Come clean now, and you will not die an agonizing death." rasped Orisis. Katsura got up, "My liege, I was going to tell you, just a little later." Orisis whacked him in his face. Katsura's lip started to bleed.

"What are you making Katsura?" Orisis asked. "Something that kills two birds with one straw" Katsura said. Orisis frowned. That was not correct. "You mean 'stone', kill two birds with one stone."

Katsura laughed. "No, my liege; I do mean 'straw'. This straw is so well aimed that it will suffice." "And these birds, who or what are they." asked Orisis. Katsura smiled; a wicked and deranged smile. "The Facce Pax and number six."

Orisis smiled "Well then, by all means, make your 'straw'."

*   *   *

Drachen was divided into a few states: Erete, in the east, Tanis in the south east, Isharti in the south west, Rangok in the west, and Epta in the north and the capital; Zorrain situated right in the middle.

Around a year after the war, Hyorin Katsura, had successfully created a magic bomb capable of destroying one third of the entire continent, and threatened to unleash it on innocent lives.

Katsura demanded that all the surviving Facce Pax be executed in exchange for the bomb not going off. Secretly however, he had another agenda. If number six really had defected, he would try to stop this. However days turned to weeks, and weeks to months. Several members of the Facce Pax had called his bluff. Number six did not show himself either.

Katsura however was not a fool. He had a contingency plan.

*   *   *

"My lord, we are awaiting your confirmation." said an officer. Hyorin Katsura stood up. Well, in reality he was sitting. However, with a mastery of magic, Katsura could project an image of himself wherever he liked.

He was on the outskirts of Helot, a fairly large city in north eastern Drachen. Hyorin Katsura looked at the city and hesitated for a moment. This was not like him. Anger flooded him, hating himself for his own weakness.

Hesitation was a sign of weakness, and weakness would not be tolerated.

"Detonate."

In less than a second, the city turned into a mausoleum. The soil was sown with sulfur and ash rained from the sky. Total deaths: thirty one thousand.

Katsura turned his back on the city. He had sent a message to the Facce Pax. Surrender, or watch the world burn.

*   *   *

The Facce Pax immediately revealed themselves. They were taken into custody and executed. Later, the people would refer to this period as 'the death of the light.'

Despite general despair, hope was not lost. The rebels, assisted by number six, conducted Operation Dragonhead. A team of elfish soldiers snuck into a Drachen fortress and managed to steal three Knaves eggs. With that the rebellion withdrew from its larger campaigns, occasionally launching small attacks.

*   *   *

Azruth, King of Tanis, was not used to being outwitted. The last time, it happened was during the war, which ended over six years ago. Being the fourth Doomknight, he had considerable sway all over Drachen. Despite this he could not catch a few rebels. This enraged him.

It had recently come to Orisis' attention that three Knaves eggs that were confiscated, were not accounted for. This led him to look into the facility where they were stored. What Orisis found instigated an uncontrollable rage in him. He set his Doomknights on high alert, believing this to be the work of rebels.

Azruth however was preoccupied. He had heard unconfirmed reports that a surviving member of the Facce Pax had been seen helping an insurgency called the Ormis Baymis. This survivor could only be identified as 'Duscuth'. The name sounded familiar to Azruth, though he couldn't remember where he had heard it.

Azruth had a theory. He believed that it was the Ormis Baymis that had stolen the egg, with help from this 'Duscuth'. Unfortunately barely had enough proof to convince himself.

Duscuth was elusive and was never in one place twice. So it was exceedingly difficult for Azruth to catch him. He frequently sent his men-at-arms on patrols where rumors of a magical tramp lived.

Duscuth would have to wait though, right now he, along with the other eight Doomknights had the problem of the eggs to deal with . . .

PART TWO
SKRALL, LAZEX AND ORISIS

It was well past midnight, Orisis Kazekage stood in the main hall of *Schatten Zorn,* the castle of the Doomknights, wearing a black armor made of dragon's scales and a complete Spartan battle helmet. In his hand was the legendary Meteor Blade. Its hilt and guard were as black as his own armor and the sleek but strong blade forged from the strongest magically enhanced metals.

He had a thin straight scar running through one of his eyes. Like the scar over his eye he had scars all over his body, from the numerous battles he had fought over the last thousand years.

Orisis was not an ordinary man. In fact, he wasn't even an extra ordinary man. For that matter he wasn't even a man. Orisis was just a manifestation. He was actually Ocathacaru; God of fear. He had been tasked with controlling the Great Evil. He was to make sure that it did not run rampant. However the fear God had played his cards well. Not only did he complete his task, but now he was a King.

Orisis had dismissed his Doomknights an hour ago, and now he was waiting. He snapped his fingers and a bone appeared in the opposite hand, he laid the bone down. Then he snapped his fingers with his other hand, and a sword appeared in his other hand. He laid it somewhat away from the bone.

He took a flask of blood out from his cloak and started drawing two complex runes, with both the bone and the sword in the middle of them respectively. The first shape was a circle with four opposite pentagons in it.

The second was a circle with two cross squares.

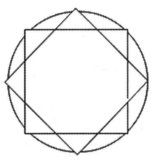

Orisis finished drawing the circles and shouted "Father Skrall, father Lazex, come forth and tell me what has happened in the hall of the Gods.

The bone and sword vanished in their missing places were two men. One was wearing the same armor as Orisis but in blood red. He also had no helmet. His face was scarred more than Orisis' and he had blond hair, pale skin and blue merciless, warlike eyes. He was Lazex; God of war.

The other man was wearing a pitch black cloak, hooded over his head, and the only thing visible on his face was two red evil eyes. He was Skrall; God of the underworld and death.

Then Skrall spoke, his voice was colder than ice and sadistic "Your elder cousin, Goddess of sleep and prophecies, Morfos, has 'spewed' one of her prophecies again." Clearly thus statement should have unsettled the Sovereign of Drachen. Orisis however, had been in the mortal world for a long time. Very few things that happened among the Gods affected him, though he was one of them. "Why would I care?" interjected Orisis.

"It's about you, and it goes a little something like this . . ." interrupted Lazex. When he spoke this time, he spoke in his true godly voice, louder and more powerful than before.

> *"'A group of four shall seek and slay*
> *One through nine they will make pay*
> *The lost ones shall be brought back*
> *Though two will have souls to lack*
> *The power of fear will be tested*
> *Or else be evenly bested*
> *Morfos' child shall grow great*
> *But in his power is not his fate*
> *If his good heart fails to win*
> *Then he will be doing many a sin*
> *The Black King will stand and fight*
> *For the mortal throne is his right'"*

"The power of fear will be tested, what the hell is Morfos thinking? NO ONE can beat me except you father," Orisis said pointing to Lazex "Or the other Gods. I can't deny the last line though; I put in some effort to build this Empire." The three were silent for a moment, and then Skrall spoke. "You are arrogant Orisis, you may be the God of fear, but prophecies are never wrong. You must know that. Prophecies from Morfos are the most dangerous. The last time she spoke one . . . well you know what happened."

"I find one of the lines a bit odd." Lazex said. "It states that the one who will challenge you will be a child of Morfos. I am not aware that there are any human children of Morfos currently alive."

"I mean no offence father, but, are you the right person to say that?" Orisis asked, slightly mockingly. Lazex was not known for his intelligence. "You are an arrogant cockroach Orisis, one day I will turn you into pulp!" Lazex shouted

"Calm down Lazex, we better get going." Skrall said, as amused as being of his affinity could be. "Oh yes, I see potential in Hyorin Katsura and Xephos Seize, maybe Lazex and I better consider having charioteers. They do have traits similar to us, after all." With that the two gods disappeared.

'*A charioteer of a god has to be a god, Lord Skrall is not thinking of . . . oh dear, he is.*' Orisis thought. He waved the thought out of his mind, but then surprisingly Skrall reappeared in front of Orisis.

"Uh, father, what do you-" but he was cut off by Skrall "Watch out for an old man called Duscuth." Then he disappeared again. '*Watch out for Duscuth he says,*' thought Orisis '*Who, by the great bloody swords of Lazex is Duscuth and why am I supposed to watch him?*'

'*Wait,*' thought Orisis *I've heard that name before. Who could have mentioned it to . . . of course that man, was Duscuth, well, he was certainly going to feel the full wrath of The Drachen Empire once he meets Ishvala again.*'

He snapped his fingers and a skeleton warrior came in. "Bring me Ishvala Negundo." said Orisis. The skeleton nodded and walked away.

PART THREE
THE RECEPTION

Duscuth was a good natured and friendly man. He was tall standing at six feet and usually wore an inexpensive dark blue robe which matched his eyes.

For six years Duscuth had managed to keep the eggs safe. For six years he had moved from city to city, desperately looking for the right kind of person. Right now, Duscuth was in the ancient city of Ilrea and he was worn.

He was living in a shack in the center of the city. It was a modest accommodation for a person of his stature. Duscuth was going over the facts in his head.

He had been running around with three eggs for six years. He was wanted all over Drachen. He was low on funds and to top it all off his horse had just died. It was truly a depressing situation.

Duscuth walked to his desk. It was the only real piece of furniture in the shack. He opened its drawer. '*Great I'm almost out of paper too.*' He thought, looking at the few pieces of parchment in his possession. He took a sheet out and began to write on it.

The letter was addressed to the Supreme Commander of the Ormis Baymis. It's gist was that Duscuth was tired of running around Drachen. After consideration he had elected to return with all three eggs. He finished off by telling the Supreme Commander that would be arriving within the month.

Duscuth stood up and read the letter. It was fine, not too casual, but he sounded firm in his choice. He tied it to his last messenger bird and let it fly.

Unbeknownst to Duscuth, Xephos Seize, King of Epta, had managed to find him. Seize quickly assembled his best knights. There was no time to call for reinforcements. He issued orders to the captain; kill Duscuth and get rid of the eggs.

The unit moved into position, they were assembled forty feet away from Duscuth's shack. The captain signaled and the knights moved in.

Duscuth heard the knights clanking and immediately moved into his escape plan. He had transport runes ready at all times. He grabbed them and laid them on the ground.

BOOM! The knights brought down Duscuth's door. They charged into the shack, but Duscuth was there to meet them. He dispatched the first two with a clever thrust turned flick. Despite his skill with a sword Duscuth was being overwhelmed. He was past his prime and he definitely couldn't take six fully trained knights on at once.

Duscuth retreated and went to get the eggs. However the knights had beaten him there. They had two eggs with them, the third lay on the ground. One of the knights carelessly charged at Duscuth and dropped the egg. "No!" Duscuth shouted. He slashed the knight and went for the others.

In the battle that followed, Duscuth single handedly took down four knights. He managed to grab one of the eggs and continued to engage what was left of the unit of knights.

One of the knights brought his sword up too high. Duscuth lunged. To shield himself the knight brought the egg in the way. Duscuth couldn't stop his sword and it pierced the shell of the Knaves egg.

Duscuth jumped back. He had just lost two eggs. Grief began to consume him. He made a run for the transport runes. He quickly lay the egg down and transferred magic into the rune. The egg disappeared.

With the egg safe, Duscuth fled.

*   *   *

Meanwhile at the Ormis Baymis headquarters, the upper echelons were in the midst of a heated debate. How would they approach the problem of the egg, and more alarmingly, there was only one egg.

The Supreme Commander was in two minds. As far as he could tell, there were two rational ways to proceed. Either they could hold on to the egg. Or they could smuggle it out of Drachen.

The Supreme Commander was not a rash man and he thought on this problem for a great deal of time. If they kept the egg within the Ormis Baymis, it could take centuries to hatch. But, if they attempted to smuggle the egg out of Drachen, they ran the risk of being caught.

The Supreme Commander shuddered, when he thought about what would happen to the person carrying the egg, if they were caught.

It was a hard choice, but to the commander it was the right one. He had decided to send the egg to Altolen. After all the Altolen was Drachen's greatest nemesis. There would be an abundance of people willing to fight Orisis there.

He just needed to find the means to get the egg there. This problem was considerably smaller than the previous one; however it was just as vital. The Supreme Commander knew he couldn't send an entire battalion to protect the egg. On the other hand, he couldn't send it with just a handful of soldiers.

Two days passed and there was still no solution at hand. However later that day The Ormis Baymis received a high priority message. The message stated the elfish lord; Kacaius was fleeing Drachen.

Kacaius was one of the few spies that Ormis Baymis had managed to slip into Orisis' government. This, though a major blow, proved to be advantageous. Lord Kacaius would be accompanied by a retinue of elves. This would ensure that the egg arrived safely in Altolen.

The Supreme Commander dispatched his fastest riders with the egg. A new era would start tomorrow.

THE HATCHING ARC

CHAPTER 1

THE EGG

Lord Kacaius and his escorts rode down to a stream. Kacaius was a tall even for an elf. He stood eight feet and three inches of the ground had blue eyes blond hair and a small blond moustache. He wore a full body chain mail suit and a long dark green cape. He was a captain in the rebellion Ormis Baymis. His mission was to smuggle the last Knaves egg outside the country and begin the [currently] non-existent Facce Pax' training.

He had ordered a halt and he and his men were in a clearing. Kacaius was happy, they had made good time. They had been riding for five days and were close to the border. The group had halted in a small clearing with a tiny stream passing through it.

Kacaius sat down under the shade of a tree and looked up at the sky. He wasn't weary, just tired. He plucked an apple from a nearby tree and began to eat it. One of his men approached him. "Sir, our scouts report that this area is frequented by Drachen patrols. They do not recommend staying here for more than half an hour. Kacaius nodded in acknowledgement and then returned to his apple.

After a twenty minute rest Lord Kacaius ordered his men to move out. The horses were saddled and the elfish company rode out of the clearing. A few minutes into the ride Kacaius began to hear something strange. The elfish lord could have sworn that he heard some twenty horses riding behind him. Reality dawned on Kacaius too late. "Break formation! Single them out!" A voice shouted from behind. Out of nowhere twenty odd mounted knights stormed into Kacaius' convoy.

The battle was over before it started. Kacaius had nine men. Normally, this would have been sufficient to take out twenty enemy soldiers. Mounted archers were one of the most valuable assets an army could have. However in the circumstances, there was nothing the elves could do.

Lord Kacaius rode hard and fast. His men knew exactly what they had signed up for. They would buy him enough time. Unfortunately time bought by others blood is seldom enough. Within minutes a few riders had caught up.

These riders weren't the heavily armored knights, but lightly equipped spearmen. Only then Lord Kacaius realized that it had been a trap. Despite his horse's best efforts the spearmen soon caught up. Lord Kacaius drew his blade for his final stand. The elfish lord was by no means a weak fighter.

Lord Kacaius was no fool however. He had a plan 'B'. It was risky and there was an excellent chance it would not work. However he had to try. In the fraction of a second before he engaged the Drachen soldiers Lord Kacaius teleported the egg to an old friend.

His old friend went by the name Duscuth and Duscuth was supposedly dead.

*   *   *

Duscuth had managed to out run several heavily armored knights. This was remarkably easier than one would think. He had gotten himself out of Ilrea and was now in the city of Thresh. Duscuth liked Thresh. He had been born just a few miles outside the city's limits.

Another bonus was that his old friend Bastonix lived here. Bastonix had been one of the few smiths brave enough to supply the Ormis Baymis with iron ore and tools. Duscuth was not planning to stay though. He had been sighted in Thresh just over a year ago.

It was actually due to Bastonix that he had a roof over his head. When he had previously been in Thresh, the smith had shown him an abandoned house. The house itself was nothing special. However it did have one great feature. Not a soul came to poke around. There were rumors going around that it was haunted. Even the soldiers feared it.

Duscuth, presently, was making himself some dinner. He opened the cabinet were he kept meat and saw the Knaves egg. '*How the hell did the Ormis Baymis find me?*' He thought. A quick look into the magic showed that Lord Kacaius had sent it. '*Ridiculous, am I that predictable?*' Duscuth thought irritably.

However maybe it was good fortune that this had happened. Bastonix's son had some magical talent. Being a smith's son he was also buff. Duscuth made up his mind. He would go to Bastonix and bring his son to the Ormis Baymis. Duscuth picked up his sheath and took to the streets.

As Duscuth was running through the streets he realized that he was being followed. "Halt!" someone shouted from behind him "Hey, you there stop running!" *'I don't have time for this.'* thought Duscuth He turned to the men approaching him. "Just my luck, it's a damn patrol." He muttered

"Hello gentlemen" said Duscuth. "You look suspiciously like that Knaves rider?" asked the sergeant gruffly. *'Damn.'* thought Duscuth, *"Elfa Simaino, Peninta, Galanos astrapes kai Brontes"* [elf spell fifty: blue thunder and lightning] he murmured. Immediately a blast of blue energy sent the patrol flying.

"What the . . ." said the sergeant in a daze. Then he collapsed. Duscuth ran until he reached a shop saying Bastonix's iron utilities. Duscuth entered the shop. The shop was dimly lit and full of isles with a great many things in them. "Bastonix," he whispered, "Bastonix."

There was no reply. Duscuth proceeded to move around the shop. At the back of the shop there was a door. Duscuth opened it. There, sitting behind a desk looking over some parchment was Bastonix Xeres.

"Good evening Bastonix." Duscuth said quietly. Bastonix looked up. His concentrated features relaxed. "Oh, Duscuth, it's you. I thought for a moment . . . well never mind. What can I do for you?"

"Where is your son?" asked Duscuth. "Upstairs. Why?" Bastonix asked, concerned. "Leon. River. Fang." Duscuth said, using a code from the Ormis Baymis. Bastonix paled, and then he nodded. "I'll close the shop."

Duscuth hurried up the small staircase. The space above the shop was very modest; three rooms. A boy sat on a cot. When Duscuth entered the room the boy looked at him. "Hey I know you, your one of my father's friends." Duscuth nodded. "Yes, I am, you need to come downstairs now." The boy got up and walked to the stairs.

"So, what's your name?" Duscuth asked as they walked down. "Dravir," replied the boy. "Dravir Xeres."

Bastonix met them when they got down. "They are coming, go now." He said gravely. Dravir frowned. "What? What is going on?" "No time to explain boy," Duscuth said. "We need to go now!"

It was at that precise moment that a small retinue of soldiers burst into the shop. "Run!" shouted Bastonix. Duscuth grabbed Dravir's arm and pulled him out the back door of the shop. "What the hell is happening?" Dravir shouted. Dusucth pulled Dravir through the back alleys of Thresh.

When the duo had gone sufficiently far from the shop, Duscuth stopped. "Listen well; I am only going to say this once. You are now a fugitive. The empire is going to come looking for us. You are of paramount importance. The hope of liberation from Orisis lives and dies with you."

Dravir stared at him. "You're crazy old man. Get away from me." Duscuth sighed. "Listen, if you want to die, you are allowed to go back to your home. However, if you want to live then you can come with me." Dravir snorted "Yeah, sure, and while I'm at it why don't I fulfill my destiny as well."

Dravir turned around and started walking back. Duscuth grabbed his wrist. "You just don't get it do you." He took the egg out. "This is the last Knaves egg in existence. It's the Facce Pax's last chance for resurrection. *You* are the last hope for resurrection. If you go back, you will be killed, just like your father."

Dravir's eyes widened. "My father is not dead." He said adamantly. "No, maybe not, but we need to get out of here right now." Duscuth said furiously. "No." said Dravir, "We have to go back for my father." Duscuth looked long and hard at him. "I'm sorry; but Bastonix knew what he was getting into. He knew what he had to do, should the situation arise."

"But-" Duscuth cut the smith's son off. "Even if we did go back for him, there is nothing we could do. Unless, you know how to take out more than fifty armed knights at once. There is nothing we can do." Dravir flared up, "That's my father you're talking about, not some prisoner."

"Take the hit and move on. If you come with me you'll be able to avenge your father." Duscuth said calmly. For some reason, these words calmed Dravir down greatly. "Alright, I'll come with you."

"Good, now let's see if we can find some horses." The pair hunted the streets until they found a man willing to sell. Duscuth paid him quickly and mounted. Dravir did the same. The two managed to get out of the city without any major hitches.

As they rode in the outskirts Duscuth asked "How much do you know about the Facce Pax?" "They were dragon riders, Orisis killed all of them." Dravir replied. "Wrong, one; the members of the Facce Pax rode Knaves, not dragons. Remember that, your Knaves will not take kindly to being called a dragon. Two; If Orisis has killed all the members of the Facce Pax, then how in Bravec's[1] name am I here."

Dravir smiled for the first time since Duscuth met him.

They rode to a nearby hill Duscuth looked around to check if they were followed. No one was there but them. He then dismounted and beckoned Dravir to do the same. "It's time to hatch your egg."

---

[1]   Bravec is the God of the Heavens and Wind. He is similar to the Greek God Zeus.

CHAPTER 2

THE KNAVES

Duscuth took out the egg. His hand was shaking "This is Hersuls." He said. "Before you become a Knaves rider, there are a few things you have to understand. One, you will respect your Knaves. Two, you and your Knaves will share a faint bond. You will be able to sense when he or she is in danger. Three, and I can't stress this enough, your Knaves will be affected by your emotions. If you undergo emotional trauma, it will have its effect on your Knaves.

Dravir nodded. "Okay, I'm ready."

"Put your hand on the egg and repeat what I say. "*Evigilabo vobis.*'" [I awake you] "It is elfish, you should know how to say this much." Dravir looked bewildered at first but then repeated. Dravir felt energy coursing through his arm. His arm began to shake. "Hold it steady." Duscuth said

The egg started to glow blue and one by one fragments of the egg started chipping off. Then a mass of neon green slime fell out of the egg and began expanding till it was roughly seven and a half feet long and three and a half feet high. Then with a flash of light the thing materialized.

The creature that hatched from the egg looked like a komodo dragon; it was grey, had two large grey dragon-like wings and large fangs.

"T . . . that is a, a dra, dragon, you're trying to kill me!" Dravir shouted. Duscuth slapped him. "What did I tell you?" The Knaves opened its mouth. Dravir braced himself for a powerful roar. He was, however was stunned by what happened next. The creature spoke. "Gentlemen, it's about time. I was beginning to think, no one would try to hatch this egg."

"Duscuth, did that Knaves just speak?" Dravir said nervously. Duscuth smiled and said "Knaves have a gift of tongues. We hear what we want to hear. Each person hears their own tongue. You and I hear the standard of Drachen. However someone from the Frostclaws would hear Barbane, their native language."

"It's true," said the Knaves "and do me a favor and please call me Hersuls."

"Alright Dravir, I see no problem with starting your training right away. You need to mount him." Dravir stared at Duscuth. "Fine, I'll show you how it's done, amateur."

Duscuth proceeded to mount and dismount Hersuls. He then explained the proper technique to Dravir. "I think I've understood.' Dravir said after a few minutes.

Twenty minutes later Dravir was sitting on Hersuls looking quite embarrassed. "In my defense," he said "it's a lot harder than it seems." Unfortunately Duscuth didn't hear. He was too busy laughing.

After he stopped, Duscuth said "First we must head north, the Dwarves of the North will forge you a sword." "Why can't we just head to the next village and buy one." asked Dravir.

"Use common sense," said Hersuls "We are now wanted by Orisis!" The Knaves had been brought up to speed. "And Facce Pax swords are different from normal ones." added Duscuth. Hersuls and Dravir stared at him.

He unsheathed his sword. "Materialize *purustas ingel!*" The blade turned black and Dravir felt that all hope had gone from the world. He felt as though all the ones he cared about suddenly left him and he could not stop them from leaving.

"My *purustas ingel* or black angel as we say drains all hope from those around me." '*Amazing*' thought Dravir. "That was horrible!" said Hersuls

"Will the Dwarves be able to make me that?" asked Dravir. "Not exactly" said Duscuth "the ability depends on your personality." "Is it possible to tell what it will do before it is forged?" asked Dravir who's excitement was increasing "Hmm . . . I'm just guessing, but I think your sword will have something to do with fire or lightning." replied Duscuth. Dravir gave him a baffled look.

"We've wasted enough time as it is," said Duscuth "let's get moving, I'll tell you the rest on the way." They walked in silence for ten minutes then Duscuth brought back the subject of swords. "You see different personalities attract different elements." "I said that your sword would be related to lightning or fire because you have an energetic personality."

Dravir nodded, that made sense to him. "You need to listen to this too Hersuls, you too will need to synchronize your fighting styles, based on this." Duscuth said

"Water swords usually have users that are carefree like the waves." He continued. "Earth swords are used by people who are stubborn. Fire goes to the rash, reckless and the unpredictable and energetic. While lightning based swords usually go to the quick witted, elusive and spontaneous. Illusion types or magic types go to the cunning and the manipulative. And finally we reach the dark swords. They generally tend to go to the people who are gloomy and anti social."

Duscuth was in his element. Words leaped out of his mouth he was going on and on till Dravir interrupted. "Why was your sword a dark type?" Duscuth's face grew dark. "It was not originally that way, I made some bad choices when I was young, don't ask me about it again."

His face returned to normal and continued on his lecture on rider swords. Leaving Dravir and Hersuls to ponder the endless possibilities of what bad choices Duscuth could have made.

Dravir was watching spellbound as Duscuth spoke about famous Facce Pax and their swords. After a while he started on the history of the Facce Pax. This bored Dravir immensely and he yearned to learn more about swords. Duscuth was talking about a rogue Facce Pax warlord when Dravir asked "Can you tell me more about swords."

Duscuth looked at him. "Alright, but on one condition," He said after a moment. "What year did the warlord Un'sarl defect from the order and form the Exodus Alliance?" Dravir gulped. "Um, well, you see it was, uh well, eh. I'm sorry I don't know." Duscuth smiled. "What about you Hersuls? Were you listening?" "Yes, I was," the Knaves said, "It was four hundred and four years ago, or 402 BO[1].

"You should have been listening Dravir." Duscuth said. "The history if the order might not be the most engaging subject, but it is important." Dravir bowed his head and apologized.

The group walked in silence for some time. Suddenly Duscuth stopped them. "Be very still." He whispered. "I think there is someone behind that tree." Sure enough seconds later a dozen arrows flew out from behind several trees. "Run!" shouted Dravir. "No, hold your positions." Duscuth said. The older man murmured something and suddenly there was a translucent shield in front of them.

Duscuth drew his blade and turned to Dravir. "Do you have anything with you?" Dravir shook his head. "No." Duscuth took out a knife from

---

[1]   BO is a standard date like: B.C. or A.D. It its full form is Before Orisis.

his robe. "Take this and don't let those soldiers see you." He shouted. In a flash the former Knaves rider was away.

The Drachen soldiers charged at them. Duscuth sliced, stabbed and slashed his way through the first few. However the soldiers retreated and spread out.

Realizing the difficulty of the situation Duscuth reasoned that he was out of options. He had to use a dangerous bit of magic that had been outlawed by the Facce Pax ages ago. *"Demonio hechizo, setenta y cuatro, Diez mil espadas!"* [Demon spell, seventy four, ten thousand swords.]

There was a loud bang then when Dravir looked again he saw of the patrol hit by black swords. In fact he saw black swords everywhere. He cast a bewildered look at Duscuth. "What in hell's name was that?" he asked

"Demon magic" Duscuth said "It is an illegal form of magic containing only the most bloodthirsty and demonic spells. "Yeah" said Hersuls "I would hate to be on the receiving end!"

Putting the horrific magic behind them, the group proceeded on. Duscuth began a conversation that slowly and awkwardly died a few minutes later. Dravir took the opportunity to ask Duscuth a question. "How do you perform magic?"

Duscuth sighed and looked at him. "Magic is a general term. It can range from being able to change the color of your hair, to being able to kill things on touch." Dravir looked slightly nervous. "What you will be learning is a set of spells labeled 'Elf Spells'. They are a set of specialized spells made for Knaves riders. They don't consume a lot of one's energy, and they don't require long rituals. They are effective in battle and have a variety of uses."

"Okay," Dravir said, "but how do you perform magic?" "Mental focus and intense concentration." replied Duscuth. The company stopped for a meal. Duscuth managed to catch some rabbits. Hersuls on the other hand, being a natural predator, took down a small deer. The Dravir grilled the rabbits over a small fire. After eating their fill, the group proceeded to continue their journey.

It was after three hours; one patrol almost finding them, and meeting four large bears Dravir began to feel hungry again. Running around the woods was more tiring than he anticipated. "Duscuth, there is a small town close, why don't we get something to eat?" asked Dravir. Dusucth looked at Dravir and then commented. "Dravir, we are fugitives, how do you think the guards are going to react if they see us strolling in."

"How large is this town, Dravir?" Hersuls asked. "Fairly large." was the reply. "That means they'll have regular patrols around the town and around it." Duscuth said. The group fell silent, thinking about the obvious problem this presented.

Suddenly Duscuth stood up straight. "What?" asked Hersuls. Duscuth smiled. "How did I not think of this before? Hersuls, you are going to fly over this town." Hersuls began to smile, or whatever a smile would look like, coming from a Knaves. Dravir was confused. "How can we manage that? Hersuls has never flown before. You expect him to carry both of us, are you crazy?"

This time it was Hersuls' turn to correct the young Facce Pax member. "We Knaves possess several gifts. The gift of strength is one of them. I can carry almost three fully grown humans on my back."

Dravir found this statement odd. "You were in an egg until this morning. How do you know this?" Duscuth opened his mouth to explain, but decided to leave it to Hersuls. "Knaves are aware of their surroundings even before they hatch." Dravir nodded, he didn't understand it, but it was a logical explanation.

It had gotten dark by that time. Duscuth looked around and said "Look Dravir, we can sit here debating and risk meeting another patrol, or we can get this over with." "Fine, let's fly over it." Dravir said. The pair proceeded to mount Hersuls. Duscuth began relaying instructions. "Hersuls, push downward with your wings. It generates more power than flapping them back and forth."

Hersuls proceeded to run and then push up off the ground. Dravir was petrified. He strongly believed that they were going to crash. However, nothing of the sort happened. Hersuls soared above the trees with the utmost control. "Still cynical?" asked Duscuth. Dravir smiled. "This is great."

When they landed, in the wee hours of the dawn, Hersuls was exhausted. They set up camp by a stream. Hersuls was sleeping under a tree while Duscuth and Dravir were out by the small hut they had built. The two men were practicing swordplay. Duscuth's immense skill, and Dravir's lack of training made it quite the one sided contest. Eventually, after several cuts and bruises, Dravir began to get the hang of it. He could now parry most of Duscuth's strokes and hold his own. Duscuth, however, was barely putting in any effort. He was purposely making it easy for Dravir.

After several more bouts, the pair stopped. Dravir was covered in sweat. He sat down on a small rock. He glanced at Duscuth. The older man had barely broke a sweat. Dravir finally decided to ask something. "Are you going to teach me elf or demon magic?" he asked.

"Both" replied Duscuth "But let's go into Elf magic first. It is comparatively easier and there won't be much damage if you go wrong." Dravir nodded. Duscuth proceeded. "In order to produce magic you need to concentrate. You must focus on what you want to manifest. In this case it will be a simple push."

Duscuth motioned for Dravir to get up. Duscuth faced the rock and muttered something unintelligible. The rock suddenly shot foreword a few feet. "This is the first Elf spell, it simply pushes something away. The incantation is 'elfa simaino ena, sprochno' [Elf spell one: push]. Try saying it once."

Dravir complied. "Elfa samhaino—wait no, Elfa simaino ena, sproco." Duscuth shook his head. "The word is sprochno, not sproco." Dravir looked slightly bashful. "If you think you have understood the words, try it out. Remember, you have to focus. Think about what you are trying to manifest."

Dravir turned toward the rock. He put his hand out and said the incantation. Nothing happened. He tried it once more. The result was the same. Dravir looked at Duscuth questioningly. "Try it one more time." Duscuth advised.

Dravir closed his eyes. He focused solely on the rock moving. He spoke the incantation. He suddenly felt a jerk on his body. He opened his eyes. Immediately he took a step back. He had somehow been transported away from their encampment. Dravir was in a place full of lava and large dark brown rocks. He was on the largest of the brown rocks and he was alone.

Suddenly a massive pillar of fire appeared ten feet in front of him. Then the fire was gone, and in its place a boy. He had fiery red skin and he was wearing light chainmail. He had a white shape on his cheek; a cross with a circle around the intersection.

He then spoke. "You have kept me waiting." His voice sounded as if 5 people were speaking. "Who are you?" asked Dravir. "I" said the boy "Am Virard, your manifestation and one of your inner spirits."

Dravir had no idea what the red skinned man was talking about. He just wanted to go back. "Perhaps an explanation is in order." Virard said. "In order to perform Elf Magic, the old Facce Pax set a test. If the apprentice could not best a manifestation of himself, he would not be allowed to continue." "So you are my test?" asked Dravir.

"In a way, yes I am." Virard replied. "However, I was not created by the Facce Pax. As I said, I am a manifestation of you. I came into being when you were born. A more common term to describe me would be 'inner spirit'." Dravir nodded, he had heard the stories about inner spirits. "You probably know that a person has three inner spirits. One represents good. One represents evil. The third represents you wholly, as in both sides.

"So who are you?" Dravir asked. "Good or evil?" Virard smiled. "Think about it Dravir. I haven't attacked you. I have answered several of your queries. And I even had the courtesy to not singe you when I appeared."

"So good" confirmed Dravir. "Good." Virard said. "Now to business, I'm sure you have realized that in order to perform Elf magic you will have to best me in combat. And no, I cannot use magic myself."

Dravir took a step back. He was going to ask if Virard could use magic. It was like the inner spirit had read his mind. "I did actually." Virard said. Dravir was shocked. It happened again. "I don't need to read your mind to assume that you are confused." Virard said coyly. "Basically, since I am a part of you, we share the same mind. I can read yours and you can read mine. I am not going to tell you how though."

Dravir opened his mouth to protest then thought better of it. Then he realized that he had thought about it. Virard laughed. "I'm the good one, remember? I won't read your mind in our duel." *'This is getting uncomfortable, do you mind if we just talk instead?'* thought Dravir. He looked at Virard. The inner spirit nodded.

"Where do we get our weapons?" asked Dravir. Virard waved his hand, an arsenal of weapons appeared. Dravir chose a sword with a red blade and silver grip and guard, whereas Virard took a sword with a white blade and a scarlet grip and guard. The two faced each other in battle stances.

"En grade!" said Virard calmly, with that they charged at each other. Dravir fought hard. Slash parry lunge block slash deflect block stab. *'Hey, I'm not that bad.'* thought Dravir. Virard raised his sword up to slash. Dravir saw his chance; he lunged and hit Virard straight in the chest.

"You beat me." he said curiously "I would be lying if I said I didn't expect this." "So now what?" asked Dravir. Virard snapped his fingers and

14

the entire place started fading away. Dravir felt the same jerk on his body as he did before and suddenly he was back at camp.

"How long was I gone?" asked Dravir to no one in particular. "Huh?" said Duscuth "You were here the whole time." He told a baffled Dravir. Duscuth smiled to himself. Only masters knew how much fun it was messing with a young apprentice's mind.

THE
DOOMKNIGHTS ARC

CHAPTER 3

THE ALCHEMIST OF LORD ORISIS

Two days after Dravir fought Virard, Duscuth decided that it was time to go to a village. "A village, are you mental? Asked Dravir "Two days ago you told me that we probably the most wanted people in the country! "I've taken that into account Dravir. I think it's worth it." replied Duscuth.

"We are going to a small village outside Tanis where a lot of Knaves eggs were found." said Hersuls. '*So he tells the lizard but not me.*' thought Dravir. He was annoyed. Hersuls had known a lot of things he didn't and it was beginning to bother him. "This place we are going to is probably the only place this side of Isharti that has a decent alchemist population. Alchemy will be used against us in combat. It is important that you know how it looks."

"Alright, if you think we should go there, then fine with me." said Dravir.

They both sat on Hersuls ready to fly. The Knaves took off from the cover of the trees. "Duscuth," asked Dravir two minutes into their flight "won't people see us if we fly in broad daylight'?" Hersuls immediately dove down. "Oh lord, I didn't think of that," Duscuth said, slightly panicked. "Wait I'll just use a spell." Dravir sighed in relief.

"*Elfa simaino tessera aoratos fragmos!*" [Elf spell 4 invisible barrier] he said. Suddenly Dravir felt a tingling sensation. When he looked down all he saw was the land below him. He felt like he was going to fall. He suddenly went slack in his seat. "Hersuls slow down!" Duscuth said. Duscuth gripped Dravir by the shoulder. "If you do that, you really will fall." Dravir sat back shakily. "Alright."

Dravir looked downward once more, to Duscuth's alarm. "This feels odd." muttered Dravir. Duscuth smiled. "I remember the first time I flew, invisible. I nearly fell off." Hersuls laughed. The two men stared at him. Sensing this, the Knaves bowed his head. "Sorry."

They flew for several hours. Idle chitchat and a few lectures by Duscuth kept the group entertained. The sun was setting when Duscuth asked Hersuls to land. He descended into a wooded area, which provided sufficient cover. The pair dismounted when Hersuls hit the ground.

"So Duscuth, what exactly is Alchemy?" Dravir asked.

"Alchemy" said Duscuth as they walked "is the manipulation of certain elements, like ice, fire, metal, etc. People drink alchemic liquid which gives there alchemic abilities a little boost. It's mainly for people who have a minimal skill with magic. There have only been two Facce Pax who have used it as their primary weapon."

"Alchemists are supervised by a council appointed by Orisis." he continued "The sovereign of Drachen has very little interest in Alchemy. The council is called the Elemental Council. Its members are under the direct employ of the Empire. They are known as 'Imperial Alchemists'. But I'm rambling on. None of this is relevant to you. All you need to know is that it isn't as effective as magic."

They walked till the edge of the wood and then stopped. "Hersuls you will have to stay here. We wouldn't want to get captured." Duscuth said. Hersuls understood. Dravir and Duscuth proceeded to walk further.

When they arrived at the town they saw a big crowd by the main road. Duscuth and Dravir walked up to one man. "Tell me my man, what is going on here, is a criminal being hung?" Duscuth asked.

"Haven't you heard?" asked the man "Ishvala Negundo is here, Lord Orisis told him that if a middle aged man called Duscuth turned up with a young boy he has to kill them, strange huh." Duscuth took a step back. *'Dear god, no.'* Dravir thought. He had heard of Ishvala, he was a Doomknight. "Duscuth maybe-" But he was cut off by the howl of the crowd.

"Here he comes!" Dravir heard someone scream. He felt a rain drop on his nose. He looked up. *'That's strange'* he thought, *'that cloud looks like a hand, and the rain is only coming from the tip of the 'fingers'.'*

"Look." he heard Duscuth say. Dravir looked back to the road. There riding a black horse was the most handsome man he had ever seen. Dravir was immediately thrown. Ishavala's appearance had utterly surprised him. The Doomknight had jet black hair and pale skin. He also wore an eye patch over his left eye He was a good six feet tall and a smile that could charm a bird of at tree.

"Don't be fooled," Duscuth told Dravir "he is the most ruthless of all the Doomknights, and he's out to kill us. When Orisis needs to persuade the public to do something, he sends Ishvala Negundo."

Ishvala was looking around and smiling at the crowd. Finally he turned to where Dravir and Duscuth were standing. He looked at them funny then he flinched. He then continued looking through the crowd. After a seemingly thorough search he spoke. It was a deep voice but not harsh. "Everyone please, I'm tired and worn please let me be today."

As if it was magic the crowd moved so fast it looked as if they disappeared. So Dravir and Duscuth were alone with Ishvala Negundo. "Duscuth, we might have a problem imminent." Dravir said quietly.

"My luck is amazing." He said. This time his voice was harsh and hard. "This is very bad" muttered Duscuth. "His Darkness, Lord Orisis said that you might be here, but I was cynical. But now, here you are. Ripe for the killing."

Ishvala drew his sword and charged, Duscuth drew his own, and the battle began slashes, slices, parries and deflects. The two fought and fought. The landscape was tearing up where the battle raged. '*And I thought I was good*' thought Dravir. But then Ishvala jumped five yards backward. Duscuth readied himself in a battle stance.

He took a flagon with a green liquid out from his cloak and drank it. Suddenly a circle of red appeared in front of his fists. "Play time's over!" he shouted. "Flame on!" The ground in 3 feet in front of Dravir spewed molten lava. The lava then hardened and separated into fifteen to twenty small puddles. Then each one rose up in the air and materialized into spikes. The spikes flew forward. "Duck!" yelled Duscuth.

'*So that's alchemy.*' thought Dravir as he dropped to the ground. Two spikes merged together and became a giant fist. The other spikes did the same. "Duck, again!" shouted Duscuth again. But Ishvala was ready for it this time. The fists dived down and hit Dravir straight into the chest.

It was pain like Dravir had not felt before. Like hot hammer whacking him in his chest. All he heard before he fainted was Duscuth shout "You piece of shit! I'm not holding back anymore! *Demonio hechizo noventa y dos Caballería od los muerto.*" [Demon spell ninety two cavalry of the dead.]

*　　*　　*

"Dravir can you hear me, Dravir." Duscuth said. He shook Dravir's body and slapped him. "What . . . oh hi Duscuth, what happened?" asked a dazed Dravir. Dravir opened his eyes, the first thing he saw was Duscuth looking at him.

He looked straight up. '*Strange,*' he thought '*that hand-like cloud with its raining finger tips hasn't left, and it's always right above Ishvala.*' He made a mental note to tell Duscuth later.

"Ishvala?" asked Dravir "Where is he?" Duscuth pointed over to where the crowd was. Forty skeletal warriors on skeleton horses were hacking and slashing at what appeared to be Ishvala Negundo.

"Come on" said Dravir, "let's get out of here while he's busy." He had a strange feeling "Nothing doing I've wanted a chance like this, a chance to kill a Doomknight for six years." Duscuth said "I am going to finish him."

"*Elfa simaino exinta ochto daimonas akontio!*" [Elf spell 68 demon javelin] he shouted. A dark maroon javelin appeared in his hand. The skeleton warriors cleared a path revealing the bloodied form of Ishvala Negundo.

Duscuth threw the javelin. It few and then hit its mark, the neck of Ishvala. Dravir watched in horror as Ishvala's head came off. The ruined form of the eighth Doomknight fell to the ground. "Now" said Duscuth "we can leave." They turned around and slowly walked back to where Hersuls had landed.

Then out of nowhere they heard maniacal and mirthless laughter.

CHAPTER 4

THE GOLDEN RETRIEVER

Dravir and Duscuth spun around. All of Ishvala's wounds had disappeared, and what appeared to be a head was emerging from what was remaining of Ishvala's neck. Dravir watched the grotesque regeneration in horror.

'Hersuls where are you, we could really use some help right now!' thought Dravir. Ishavala got up and stated laughing like he was insane. "What the hell is going on?" he asked Duscuth

Duscuth's face lost all the color it still had. "How is this possible. We killed him. He was decapitated. How can he just get back up?" asked Dravir "Now is not the time." whispered Duscuth.

"Well if the old man won't tell you, I will." shouted Ishvala whose head had now completely reappeared. "Instant regeneration. Over the years I have experimented on myself. A few years ago, I found the perfect substance for regeneration. I am now indestructible. It's only a matter of time before I am appointed the First Doomknight."

Dravir's face was paler than the moon. He was facing an enemy that couldn't be killed. Dravir couldn't see any possible way out of this. He looked at Duscuth. "We carry on." The older man said. Ishavala chuckled. "How cute. You think you can kill me. I find it comical." He took out another flask from his cloak. "I am a Doomknight, you fool! Now it's time for you to die."

"Over my dead body!" shouted a voice somewhere behind them. *'Hersuls!'* thought Dravir and he spun around. There was Hersuls flying above them. He swooped at Ishvala and opened his mouth and sent a large blast fire point blank at Ishvala.

Ishvala screamed in agony. The fire was doing its job. It took a couple seconds for it to die out. Ishvala's clothes were in tatters. He wiped the blood off his lip and then snarled. "Bastard, even though I can't die doesn't mean that I don't feel pain. Duscuth charged at him, but Ishvala was too fast. The Alchemist created a sword of fire. He then lunged digging the sword into Duscuth's thigh. "Shit!" shouted Dravir

But then someone slashed him out of nowhere. "No," gasped Ishvala "no, I'm doing my mission and I'm succeeding, no not him, not you!" The Doomknight was spouting gibberish. It was as if there was an invisible man standing in front of him. Then that old confidence came back. Ishavala waved his sword around. It looked like he was trying to slash someone who wasn't present.

Suddenly green light erupted from the sky. Some of the buildings close to Ishvala were starting to break down. Then three black flashes appeared in the sky. Two cloaked figures descended down to the ground. The third, still in the air threw off his cloak.

The man was wearing a thin gray-gold armor and leggings. He wore a cape of midnight black, his face was painted black except a red circle that started above his nose and ended right under his mouth. Everything in that circle was red. On his head was a helmet that was as black as obsidian, it looked like a Spartan helmet without the colorful mohawk at the top.

The man was holding a pure white walking stick which made him look like someone important waiting for something. Then he smiled, not a warm happy smile but a bloodthirsty and vicious smile. This man's presence was so intimidating, it was like he was emanating bloodlust.

Dravir and Hersuls were standing transfixed at the man. The man snapped his fingers and the two shadows lifted Ishvala Negundo and disappeared.

After the man left Dravir regained some of his sense, he ran over to Duscuth. Somehow the wound was not that serious. "Who was that man?" asked Dravir. "That man" whispered Duscuth "is Lord Hyorin Katsura, the second Doomknight or the golden retriever."

CHAPTER 5

SCHATTEN ZORN

Dravir took Duscuth to the nearest house to tend to his wounds. The people were more than compliant when they saw Hersuls.

*   *   *

Lord Hyorin Katsura was walking through the doors of *Schatten Zorn,* the greatest fortress in Drachen. *Schatten Zorn* lay in a small state called Zorrain. Even though Zorrain was a small state it was the second most important state in Drachen, preceded by Epta.

It was a large dark gray castle with four towers, one at each end. In between the towers was a large square dome. Easily the largest building in the Drachen Empire, it could be seen for miles around. It dominated the landscape, reminding the people of Orisis' rule.

Katsura stood before a pair of large bronze doors. This was the entrance to *Schatten Zorn.* The doors themselves could only be opened from the inside. So there were always a few soldiers posted in the castle. Atop the doors a banner flew; a black dragon on a field of white. It was the symbol of Orisis, and inspired fear everywhere. There were two guards standing in front of the door. As soon as they saw him they snapped to attention.

One of the two looked up and shouted "It is Lord Hyorin Katsura, open the gates!" The Doors slowly creaked open. His two shadows glided into the castle carrying the broken form of Ishvala Negundo.

They were in a beautiful garden now, full of large silver trees and small flowers. But Hyorin Katsura paid no attention to it. He went through a number of rooms, until he reached two golden doors with the words *hall of Orisis* etched on then.

Under that there were nine swords facing downward, each with a number from one to nine, each sword's hilt was a different color. The first was crimson, the second was light green, the third was maroon, the fourth was purple, the fifth was navy blue, the sixth was the color of frost, the seventh was white, the eighth was turquoise and the nine was dark orange.

Strangely number eight kept fading and unfading. Hyorin knocked on the 'two sword' five times. Then the double doors opened to reveal a table with two empty seats.

At the head of the table was Lord Orisis, tall and well built with a bored expression on his face. On the first side seat on his right sat Xephos Seize, taller than Orisis. Seize seemed to be in deep conversation with the man next to him; Shrukin. The first side seat on the left was left empty. He knew that that was his chair.

Slowly he strode over to the table and he pulled out his chair and sat down. "Now" Orisis rasped "that Hyorin Katsura has finished with his little job I believe we have matters to discuss." Orisis paused, looking at the Doomknights. "I must tell you that, Hyorin Katsura has seen the young Facce Pax"

"Also, our beloved Drachen Empire suffered a heavy blow yesterday courtesy our Hevgee neighbor." he continued. "Commander Horus Stratzee was struck down along with three hundred other irregulars by our Hevgee friends." Orisis let this statement sink in.

"I propose that we eradicate all citizens of Hevgee decent in Drachen!" Someone said from the back of the table. It was Roy Cyphrure. He had light brown skin which made it seem that he was from Epta, and light blue hair. He had a scar from this forehead through his eye and down till his chin. He has frosty blue eyes that were battle hardened and mean looking.

"Imbecile such a move would provoke mass rebellion, but," interrupted Orisis "right now we have another important matter at hand; our friend here has failed his mission." He gestured toward where Ishvala stood. "All those in favor of his execution raise your hands!" Six hands went up. "Hyorin Katsura, as expected. Shrukin, Azruth, oh Edmund; you're usually one to keep people alive. Zayal of course, and Mietitore. Ah good now we have a ruling, kill him!"

There were no murmurs, which usually accompany the sentencing. For they were Doomknights. Each one of them glorified war and lived by sheer aggression.

"Wait," said Orisis just when it seemed Ishvala's fate was sealed. "Katsura, you have got the chance you have wanted, take the fluid, and be quick about it." Hyorin Katsura got up and walked toward the body. "The puppet master, he's going to kill me!" croaked Ishvala startling everyone at the table.

Katsura slashed the eye patch off with his walking stick. He took a flask from his cloak and set it down next to him. He then drew a knife. Ishavala's eyes widened. Katsura knew about the regenerative fluid. The second Doomknight grabbed Ishavala's wrist. He then mercilessly cut it. Blood seeped out. Katsura calmly took the flask and filled it. He then kicked the body to the ground and then returned to his chair.

"With any luck, I will be able to reproduce it in a year." Katsura said uncertainly.

Orisis snapped his fingers, two cloaked skeletons holding large, murderous axes rose from the ground. "Take him outside" he said pointing at Ishavala. "And send someone to clean up this blood." The skeletons nodded and took the former Doomknight outside.

"Now Hyorin" said Orisis "please tell us about our new Facce Pax." Katsura chortled "Why do you want to know about that insignificant piece of trash?" Orisis glared at him. "All right, all right, he's a total weakling, looked as if he hasn't performed a single spell in his life. He relies on his Knaves and the old man too much."

Orisis closed his eyes. The Doomknights knew better than to interrupt. After five minutes of silence he opened his eyes and spoke "They are heading north, to the land of the Dwarves; the old man wants him to get his rider's blade. I want Siphon, McHale and Eragor to deal with them; he should be dead by the time I wake up tomorrow!"

Another man got up. His skin was pure white; he had a pair of black horns on his head. He had one eye right above his nose and two large fangs that stretched down to his chin. He wore dark grey battle armor. "My lord" he rasped, his voice was cold and made you feel as if someone was breathing on your neck. "As the demon king I will be able to summon them now, much less time and effort wasted."

"Very well" boomed Orisis "I want to give them one extra instruction, a little surprise for our young friend and his Knaves." Orisis stood up and ordered the leave. "Oh yes, Azruth, they are still in your territory, do your best to thwart him, send Duroza and Thardison after them or something."

CHAPTER 6

THE PLOT OF NUMBER THREE

Shrukin was in his study in castle Temjuin. The room was made of wood and stone. He had a fire pit and a marble table in the study. On that table there was a board with the entire map of the world on it. There was one piece on it, right on the location of *Schatten Zorn*.

"Damn him," Shrukin muttered, "he had to go get himself killed by failing his mission didn't he? I had to vote to kill him, because Hyorin Katsura scared the wits out of him and the spell broke, which shattered my control."

"I want that power so much it is unbelievable." murmured Shrukin, he rarely talked to himself. He loathed Orisis and the other Doomknights. He wanted to crush them. "I'll obtain that power somehow and soon, Orisis will become a puny human without and I will rule the world for eternity!"

"My lord" said a voice behind him "Why don't you turn some of the other Doomknights into your puppets." Shrukin turned around. The voice belonged to girl of around twenty five. She was tall had brown hair and pale skin. Her appearance fooled you as she was a talented warrior and sorceress with a fierce temper that she only controlled in the presence of Doomknights.

"My dear Cassandra, Orisis or, Ocathacaru, must be surrounded by the people whose minds I control and you know I dare not try it on Seize or Katsura." replied Shrukin. "But my lord if you want his power you should take it by force." said Cassandra. "Force, that is the problem, Orisis has so much force that even without the Doomknights, or for that matter the army, he could take down all three parts of this continent." muttered Shrukin

"My lord you have a few high ranked people under your mind control, Commander Stratzee, Colonel Mulcivan, General Lecronom, and others."

said Cassandra. "Stratzee is dead, Mulcivan is campaigning in Altolen right now, so only Lecronom remains useful." moaned Shrukin.

"What about the legendary Shadow Jewel in the elfish forests?" suggested Cassandra. "The Shadow Jewel, it is supposedly able to grant untold power and magic to anyone who possessed it." Shrukin muttered to himself. "Good idea, I could become immortal and all powerful." exclaimed Shrukin.

"It is time for the Drachen Empire to feel the full power of my manipulation." he said with a mirthless laugh. He waved his hand and new pieces appeared o the board. One in Altolen, one in Isharti and five spread out over Zorrain.

"It is time to make more puppets!" said Shrukin "Cassandra please bring Lieutenant General Jurga, Lord Castel and Grazen, Trez and Valhallus of the Black Shadows to me."

"My lord if I may ask, why Castel, Grazen, Trez and Valhallus?" asked Cassandra. "Because Castel is a Commander in our ranks and Valhallus despite being a Black Shadow is also a War Advisor, Orisis trusts his judgment too much for my liking. Look for the obvious for the other two."

"Very well my lord." she answered. "And how will we obtain the Shadow Jewel?" "Send a squadron of men to the Elfish forests, surrender or death." said Shrukin.

"If our first attempt fails then I will enter the fray myself and make the elves sorry that they hid the jewel from me." said Shrukin. "There are three elfish forests. Where do we look?" asked Cassandra. Shrukin opened his mouth to say something, but then slowly closed it. "That" he said "is a very good question." Cassandra laughed.

THE DWARVES ARC

CHAPTER 7

THE DWARVES OF THE NORTH

As the Doomknights were leaving Orisis' meeting room Dravir and Duscuth were thanking the owner of the house. "I didn't want to do this but it seems necessary." grumbled Duscuth "Huh?" questioned Dravir. "We'll have to fly to the north and that will tire Hersuls." He continued. "But first we have to get you a better temporary weapon."

"There were some good looking swords in the market." said Dravir "And I have a little money with me." Duscuth stared at him. Dravir knew what that meant. He turned around and ran.

He came back two minutes later holding a broadsword. It was shiny and strong. "That'll do you good in a fight." remarked Duscuth as he performed some strokes mid air. They walked into the woods. Hersuls had disappeared after he knew Duscuth was going to be fine. Both Dravir and Duscuth had a hunch that he was out here.

There was a cool breeze in the woods. Duscuth and Dravir wandered around calling out for Hersuls. After twenty minutes of searching they found Hersuls drinking water from a small creak.

"What took you so long?" the Knaves asked. "Nothing relevant. We just couldn't find you." Duscuth answered. He motioned for Hersuls to come closer. We are going to have to fly directly to the Dwarves. We can't go by foot any longer. We'll risk running into larger patrols or even another Doomknight." Hersuls and Dravir agreed. The plan made sense to both of them. "However there is a flaw in this plan. Hersuls, you will be physically strained." "I don't mind." Hersuls said. "Good man." Grunted Duscuth

Dravir mounted Hersuls. When Duscuth tried however, he gave a sharp cry. "Are you alright?" Dravir asked, as he jumped off Hersuls. "I am fine. Why did I have to get stabbed in the thigh?" Duscuth said, determined to get this over with. He carefully mounted Hersuls, ignoring the searing pain in his thigh. He let out a sigh when he sat atop. "That's more like it." Dravir mounted and Hersuls took off.

The next two days were almost identical, wake up early in the morning so that the owner of the establishment wouldn't catch them, flying for some six hours, then, finding some secluded part of the woods to practice. They would then eat some of the game that Duscuth had caught and cooked. Then it was to a farmhouse or old inn to sleep.

On the third day, Dravir remembered the strange cloud he had seen above Ishvala. When they were in the air he asked. "Oh, um Duscuth," "I saw a cloud over Ishvala, it looked like a hand. Rain was falling from the 'fingers'. What was it?"

If Duscuth had an answer he didn't reply because jut then a large shard of ice flew up missing Hersuls head by inches. "Land now!" shouted Duscuth. Hersuls did not need to be told twice. He dive-bombed straight toward the ground.

There were three figures down below as Dravir could see it. One red, one icy blue and one yellow, Hersuls was twenty feet from the ground when the red figure threw a large red ball of fire. "Aaaaaaaah!!!!!!!!" screamed Dravir. He closed his eyes.

Dravir felt Hersuls landing within seconds. He opened his eyes as soon as he knew that they were on solid ground. The three figures in front of him were definitely non-human. For one they were at least ten feet tall, had large fangs and one horn sprouting out of their foreheads.

"Chi demons, damn it. Orisis knows where we are going!" Duscuth muttered. The blue Chi demon moved in front of its brethren. "Would you be Duscuth?" he asked sarcastically. Duscuth didn't reply, but said "Dravir run away now, you won't stand a chance against three chi demons."

"Not this time." shouted Dravir "I'm staying and fighting." He unsheathed his sword. The Chi demons smiled. The red one took out a six foot sword; the blue one took out a thin but sharp katana the size of Duscuth and the yellow one took out a giant club.

"I forgot to introduce ourselves to your little friend, Duscuth," the blue chi demon said with a sneer. "I'm Lethe Eragor, Chi demon of ice. He is Phlegethon McHale, Chi demon of fire" he said pointing at the red creature "and that's Acheron Siphon, the Chi demon of lightning. We are the three Chi demons of the Underworld."

"Very nice but, we have our orders, let's crush them" said Siphon. He brought his club up in an instant, and smashed down just as fast, right where Duscuth was standing. The force of the smash was so much that Dravir, standing ten feet away from the club was thrown of his feet.

"Hersuls!" he shouted "Can you take care of McHale?" "Sure!" the reply came. Hersuls flew up and started harassing McHale, hitting him with fire then flying out of reach.

Dravir's only thought was Duscuth. He hadn't studied the theory for anything over elf spell ten, but desperate time called for desperate measures. He was relying on sheer luck and memory. *"Elfa simaino trianta exi diplos fotia!"* [Elf spell 36 dual fires]He shouted.

Two blasts of scarlet fire blasted out at Eragor. BOOM! The fires hit him straight in the chest. The Chi demon fell down with a loud 'thud!' Siphon turned towards him. "Why you little pest!" he roared. He took his club back to strike for the kill. Dravir was terrified. He tried to run but his feet were stuck.

Then he heard it; half dozen dull twangs. Siphon looked behind him. McHale was running toward him yelling. There were six arrows and scorch marks on his back. Siphon jumped back three feet to where Eragor was. He put two fingers up in front of his face and disappeared.

Dravir realized that McHale had also vanished. He turned toward the source of the twangs. There were a dozen small people with large beards and dressed in bronze armor standing there wielding battle-axes and bows.

"Good riddance" The one standing in the front said. Then he turned around and bellowed orders to some others. They ran over to Duscuth and picked him up and took him over to their little group. Hersuls landed by him. "Who are they?" he asked

The man who had been standing in the front came up to him. He had a reddish beard and had on a silver war helmet, and, "Come with me lad," He said "I'm Tyr, and we're Dwarves of the north."

CHAPTER 8

THE HALLS OF THE MOUNTAIN KING

Tyr led Dravir through a small wood. As they walked Dravir realized that the Dwarves were not as small as he originally thought. Actually they were around four and a half feet tall. They were tough and hardy. Their oddest characteristic was not their height as most people believed. It was actually their beards. From what Dravir understood, dwarves were born with them. The beard changed color as the dwarf aged.

Dravir had never been in the presence of dwarves before. He was therefore naturally curious. He had heard great things about the dwarves, though he doubted that they were all true.

"So" Dravir asked Tyr "Is it true that dwarves have more gold for themselves than the King of Epta?" "Gold?" snorted Tyr "Lad, we have plenty of gold, but not in those proportions. Gold; however is only our second favorite substance." Dravir's eyebrows rose. He hadn't heard of this before.

"We dwarves are skilled at crafting with metals, but our favorite are pearls." "Pearls?" questioned Hersuls.

Tyr gazed up into the sky with a dreamy expression. "Yes well, they are a good jewel, very hard to get." He said blushing "Oh, we are here already, that, is the rock of Aminas" he said hastily changing the subject.

They had been talking so much that they did not realize that they were standing in front of a forty foot tall rock with a mountain range behind it. [Which they could barely see] Tyr walked up to it and knocked. A small part of the rock opened. Two eyes were looking out. Tyr and the dwarf-in-the-rock conversed in Dwarfish. Dravir only recognized two words because they were in the standard of Drachen; Duscuth and Knaves.

The slit in the rock disappeared and a door appeared. Tyr gestured to go in. The door was small and not at all wide. Dravir had to duck while entering and Hersuls couldn't enter at all. "Oh sorry" said the Dwarf by the entrance. He pressed some buttons by his table and the rock mass at the side of the door parted, making the entrance wider. The doors were now wide enough for Hersuls to enter.

The tunnels by contrast were quite wide. The tunnel they were walking through looked like a cave. There were braziers on both sides every few feet. Colorful tapestries showing different metals and swords and feasting dwarves hung on the cave walls.

After walking a couple minutes Dravir felt like he was walking upward. The tunnel was ending, Dravir could see light ahead. "Finally!" exclaimed Hersuls "An end to these cursed tunnels." Tyr gave him a dirty stare.

The party stopped abruptly. Dravir looked up; there was only a few steps worth of cave left. Ahead was an open rope bridge. They were up in the mountains. There were log cabins and rope bridges littered all over them. It was a truly beautiful scene. Hersuls said something to Tyr that Dravir couldn't hear. "Not only that: Animas also has incredible strategic value." Tyr said, back to the Knaves.

"Wow" murmured Dravir. They walked on the bridge while Hersuls flew to the other end. They were on a circular platform now. There were five different bridges. "You'll be coming with me, and Duscuth will be heading to the infirmary." said Tyr. He stepped on the rope bridge in the middle. Dravir followed with Hersuls flying above him.

"Hey Hersuls" asked Dravir looking up at him. "Where do you think we are going?" "I don't know" answered Hersuls. "Probably to their leader's palace, but if you really want to know ask Tyr, I've never been here." Dravir looked back down. What he saw before him took his breath away.

A large palace lay ahead of them. The palace was built in the side of a mountain and was majestic and beautiful. There were engravings of scenes of battle and a Dwarf sitting on a throne and a forge with Dwarves around them. The skill of the carvers was done complete justice by this titanic monument.

They kept their pace and soon were at its large metal gates. There were four exceptionally large dwarves stationed there wielding spears and shields. Tyr walked up to one of them, who Dravir guessed to be the leader. They conversed quickly in Dwarfish. The dwarf then shouted something that Dravir couldn't comprehend.

He looked at Hersuls who looked equally puzzled. He turned to Tyr who mouthed one word: *open*. The large metal doors opened revealing a dark hall with a red carpet and oil paintings.

"Welcome" said Tyr "to the hall of the Dwarf King." They walked along the carpet until they reached a large brass doors. Tyr pushed them open the doors. They were in a large rectangular room. There were Dwarf guards all over the place. Right against the back wall were solid gold stairs that led eight feet in the air. At the end to the stairs there was gold throne and on that throne sat the Dwarf King.

He had countless scars on his face, his eyes were gold and he was wearing gold armor. He had darkish skin; his body was ripped with muscles from working long hours in the forges and he had a broken nose.

"Who are you, and why have you come to Aminas?" he asked. His voice was very deep, as if the earth itself was talking. "I" said Dravir walking forward "am Dravir Xeres, Facce Pax, apprentice to Duscuth, son of-" he was cut off by the Dwarf king. "You talk too much son. I am Odin, king of the Dwarves of the North. Tell me what you are doing here." Dravir plunged into the events that happened in the past weeks.

"I see," bellowed Odin "so you want an official Facce Pax blade, well you will have one, on one condition." Dravir raised an eyebrow. "My spies" continued Odin, "report that the Orcs are going to invade in around two months from now, I want you to help us fight."

"Deal!" said Dravir "Very well!" bellowed Odin who looked like he had shed a bit of excess burden. "Tyr give escort them to their apartment." "Yes my lord." said Tyr. The trio bowed and walked out of the hall.

"Charming fellow, your King, how old is he, if I may ask?" Dravir asked. "Eighty seven," Tyr said without stopping. That shocked Dravir. The King may have looked weary, but he definitely did not look that old. "But then," Tyr said. "That would probably be forty five in human terms."

They reached another one of those circular platforms. Tyr led them onto another rope bridge. They walked some more. "Just a little further, I have a feeling you will like your living quarters." Tyr said. A few minutes later they arrived at a two story house. It was large and made of wood. "This is one of the few quarters we have for people your size. I think you will find it pretty comfortable." Tyr said pointing at the house.

"I could get used to this." said Dravir.

CHAPTER 9

THE INJECTION OF EVIL

A day later Duscuth had joined them in the apartment. The dwarves had taken care of his injuries from Siphon. They also gave him something for his thigh. There was a lot of light and plants in the cabin. The day after Duscuth returned training resumed. Dravir resumed learning elf magic. In addition to this Duscuth and a few dwarves taught him swordplay.

That night he told Duscuth the deal he struck with Odin. "I was told by Odin. He called me after my wounds healed." "It should be easy right? Aren't Orcs human sized?" he asked. Duscuth gave him a look that made Dravir regret what he had just said.

"They are roughly the size of Chi demons." He finally replied. Dravir looked at him with complete horror. "They've got green skin and fangs. Some of them can spray acid from their mouths and they are fast as hell."

"We can only hope that" he continued "Odin has sufficient men to deal with this. His spies reported a host of six thousand has been assembled. They left the Peak of Fire nine days ago." He turned to Dravir "I'm going to increase your daily elf spells to ten, and it can't hurt to know demon spells one to forty five."

There was a small field behind their cabin, so they practiced sword fighting and magic. Pretty soon Dravir had memorized elf spell one to eighty. Finally the day arrived when Duscuth allowed Dravir to start Demon magic.

"The same thing will happen like last time, you will enter your inner soul and fight, this time, your good half, and your bad half will be more aggressive so keep on your toes." Duscuth told Dravir before they started. *"Demonio hechizo un la roza espada!"* [Demon spell one: slashing sword] shouted Dravir. He closed his eyes and allowed himself to be taken to his inner soul.

When he opened his eyes he was back at the place where he met Virard, but here the lava around him was black and the rock he was standing on was blood red. "I like Virard's place much better." he muttered.

BOOM! A black figure stood ahead of him. He was at least ten feet tall, he had red fangs. He had snake-like eyes which were yellow and he had huge muscular forearms. He was holding a half red, half black sword. On the top of his left arm he had the same white shape as Virard did on his cheek.

Then he stabbed. Dravir cried out in pain. Then the creature spoke; "I am the phantom of fire, the king of the flames, the master of all destruction a flame can do! I am Blaze! Get up Dravir so I can beat you to the ground again."

Dravir slowly got up; the pain in his side was incredible. "Weapon . . ." he croaked. Blaze turned towards him and threw a sword. Dravir got up and brought the sword up into a defensive position.

Blaze charged hacking and slashing the landscape as he ran. The two swords met in the air with a loud bang. Blaze's power was ferocious. Dravir struggled to repel his attacks. He could only hope to deflect them, as parrying or trying to block would be suicide.

Blaze brought his sword down in a deadly arc which missed Dravir by an inch but smashed the ground in front of him. Dravir was thrown off his feet and fell to the ground. Blaze loomed over him, his sword above his head ready to slice his head into two.

Dravir jumped to his feet thrusting his sword into Blaze's stomach. Blaze staggered backward. He waited for Blaze to snap his fingers and he be transported back the real world.

No such thing happened. Blaze stopped staggering and thrust his sword into Dravir's heart. "You think I'm on the same level as you or Virard?" He said with disgust. "Well remember this boy, you may be able to perform demon magic now but I can't be suppressed. I beat you!"

He snapped his fingers and Dravir felt his wounds closing up. He was going back. The last thing he saw was Blaze's sneer. He closed his eyes and allowed himself to return to the world mentally. Duscuth would know how to fix this, Duscuth could help him.

Dravir felt a cool breeze on his cheek. He opened his eyes knowing he was back. Duscuth stood a few feet away from him. "So, how'd it go?" he asked "I lost." Dravir said putting a lot of emphasis on lost.

Duscuth simply stared at him, "So what happens now, do I get a second chance?" asked Dravir "There is no second chance." Duscuth said quietly. "So what happens now?" asked Dravir his hope slowly fading. Duscuth opened his mouth to answer but nothing came out. Then his face started gaining color. "Hmm . . . when it comes to thing like this I usually have," he said "no idea whatsoever," he put in cheerfully

"Oh yeah Odin sent a messenger to me while you were out, your blade is ready." He told a crestfallen Dravir, "Cheer up Dravir, I'm sure they'll be no lasting damage," he said. Duscuth had no idea how wrong he was.

THE ORC INVASION ARC

CHAPTER 10

MORFOS' HELLFIRE PART 1

"What?" said Dravir instantly looking up. "My blade is ready! That's great news! When can I get it?" Duscuth smiled. He remembered when he was given his blade. "Right now if you want." said Duscuth, relieved that Dravir's gloom had left. Dravir sped towards the cabin, but then stopped, "Um, Duscuth, where exactly am I going?" he asked.

Duscuth chuckled, "Young people, how funny can they get. You're going to the forges." "Right." said Dravir. He turned around and started running, but stopped again. "Uh, Duscuth where exactly are the forges?"

"You're a master of direction." said Duscuth sarcastically. "Come on I'll show you." They walked into the cabin and called Hersuls. The left the cabin and walked on a bridge for some time, then they took a left, then a right, two more lefts and finally a right. Ahead was a large metallic building with swords, spears and scenes of battle.

"How do you know how to navigate around here, you were in the infirmary for sometime while we were in the cabin." asked Hersuls. "Think about it Hersuls, who are the only people who can make rider swords? What do I have hanging on my belt?" answered Duscuth.

"So you came, and, oh I get it now!" Hersuls exclaimed. "Eureka." said Duscuth under his breath. He and Dravir both laughed all the way at seeing Hersuls' baffled face.

Unlike the palace there only one small door, which was thankfully just big enough for Hersuls to fit in, with a bit of a squeeze. The room was large and had several doors around it. In the center was a large gray anvil. Tyr along with two other Dwarves was standing by the anvil talking in Dwarfish.

Duscuth cleared his throat. The Dwarves turned to face them. "Ah yes we'll be going into that door." said the Dwarf on Tyr's right. He pointed to a rusty looking door. "It hasn't been used since you came, Duscuth, that was twenty years ago, before 'it' happened." he continued. Dravir saw Duscuth's face go dark just like the time when he had asked about his sword.

The company walked toward it. There were two marks on the door one at the top and one on the bottom. The one on the top was two triangles with opposite ends with a crescent moon in it.

The other one was a diamond with a four point star on it.

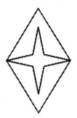

Tyr must have sensed that Dravir was looking at them so he quietly came while the other Dwarf was opening the door. "The one on the top" he told a startled Dravir "is the mark of Simain the goddess magic and wisdom, and the one on the bottom is the mark of Ironia goddess of metal and forging. It's natural to be interested in them because of the power the marks radiate."

"It's not like that, it's just that I have a mark like those on my back." said Dravir. Everyone in the party froze. "Dravir, for how long have you had this mark?" asked Duscuth in a quiet voice. "I've had it since birth." Dravir replied. "Remove your shirt." whispered Tyr.

Dravir obeyed, he took off his shirt and pointed to where the mark was. It was exactly like the one on Virard's cheek and Blaze's shoulder except it was lime green.

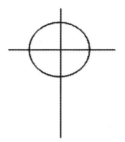

"The mark of Morfos." gasped Tyr. "Hail Dravir, son of Morfos, goddess of sleep and dreams!" said Tyr and the other two Dwarves in unison. Dravir was feeling nervous so he decided to change the subject. "Where's my sword?"

The Dwarves, still in shock of Dravir's true identity pointed toward the door. With Dravir leading the party marched straight into the room. Like the bigger one had an anvil in the center, but this time the anvil had something on it: a sword!

Before Dravir could grab it, Duscuth stopped him. "You're taking this quite well. Did you know who your mother was?" "No." Dravir replied. "But I always assumed it was something like that. Father could never explain about who my mother was. Whenever I asked, he looked up at the sky and mumbled 'what do I tell him?'"

Duscuth nodded. The gods occasionally had children with mortals. This story was not uncommon. "Now can I have my blade?" asked Dravir.

"It just needs one more thing" said Tyr looking at Dravir "your blood." Duscuth handed him a knife. Tyr took a small cup and said "Let the blood flow out till the cup is filled. Dravir raised the knife over his hand and brought it down.

A sudden flash of green light stopped him. The cup was full of blood and there was not a single wound on Dravir. Then Tyr exclaimed as he saw a piece of parchment in the cup. He took it out read it and gave it to Dravir. The parchment had only eleven words on it.

The creation of Lazex and Skrall must be removed from this world.

The note was signed by Morfos. He gave the note to Duscuth not knowing what it meant. Duscuth pondered over it for a long time, and then he realized something.

"I am sure" he said "that you are well aware of Lazex the god of destruction, hate, deceit, and of course war. I am also sure that you know of Skrall the god of the underworld. Finally," he continued "I am more than sure that you know of Lord Orisis Kazekage." Dravir raised an eyebrow.

"Sit down," said Duscuth. "has anyone ever told you how the god of fear was created." Seeing that Dravir looked as if he had no idea about what he was talking about, Duscuth went on.

"The god of fear is Ocathacaru; he was not born but created by two male gods, who of course are Skrall and Lazex. They made him in the image of an ancient king. One who was so great that he took the heavens for twenty three days and twenty three nights: The Black King; Isis." The dwarves shuddered at the name. "Necromantic energy from Skrall, infused with the remains of the Black King created Ocathacaru."

"Ocathacaru's better known alias is Lord Orisis Kazekage."

Dravir sat upright as soon as Orisis' name was mentioned. 'So,' thought Dravir 'my mother wants me to kill Orisis, but wait, a god can't be killed, or can they?'

"Duscuth what does my mother mean by remove him?" asked Dravir "Whilst a god is on this world in a human body like Orisis he can be removed by killing his mortal body." he replied.

'If that's what she wants' thought Dravir 'that's what I'll do, or at least die trying.' But then his attention returned to his sword. "So what do we do now?" he asked "Well" said Tyr "We pour this on your sword."

He picked up the cup and poured the blood all over the sword. The entire blade turned to fire then reformed.

The blade was tinged red but the hilt stayed the same: brown with leather support. In all it looked exactly like Duscuth's but the blade was tinged red and not tinged black. There was the mark of Morfos right where the iron blade stated, which was glowing.

"So" asked Dravir "what is its ability?" he was eager to see what element it was. "We'll find that out when we get back to our field." "It looks like a red toothpick." said Hersuls scaring the living daylight out of everyone. With all the commotion they forgot he was there. Dravir gave him a mean look and Hersuls understood that the sword was his pride and joy.

CHAPTER 11

THE CRIMSON BLUR

Two months breezed by, Dravir had learned the art of swordplay to Duscuth's satisfaction. He also began to learn the basics of swordplay while riding Hersuls.

Dravir had finally found out what his blade was called and what it did. So Duscuth had made him start practicing with it. He gave his old sword to the Dwarves as a gift. Contrary to what Dravir had believed, using the ability of his sword was actually tough work. It physically exhausted him and drained whatever magical reserves he had.

The atmosphere in Aminas, however was quite tense. It had been two months since the trio's arrival. The Dwarves of the North were preparing for war.

Scouts were reporting seeing small scouting parties of Orcs moving closer to Aminas. Duscuth took it as a reason to polish his apprentice's skills. He was drilling Hersuls and Dravir more than he ever had.

"Right Dravir activate your sword and shoot out a wall of flames ten times." Duscuth said. The group was out on the field. "Hersuls, fly the course I set in the hills twice with the rider dummy. Odin has called me so don't stop practicing while I'm gone."

Dravir rolled his eyes. Duscuth was being a drill sergeant. Over the last month and a half he built up strength. It no longer drained him as much. He drew his blade. It had taken a week for him to figure out its name: *Gehenam*

"Roar, *Gehenam"* [hellfire] the mark of Morfos burned the color of fire and consumed the entire blade, he pointed his sword forward *"Sacer ingnis murum!"* [Wall of cursed fire] he shouted. A large wall of green flames erupted from the poise and shot out with blinding speed.

Duscuth walked away. He walked through the cabin and reached the bridge he took a left then a right but stopped dead in his tracks. Standing on top of a high mountain ten feet from where Duscuth stood was Xephos Seize.

"Now, now Duscuth I haven't come here to kill you." He said. His voice was drawling as if someone was walking on your grave. Great warriors went mad by just hearing that voice. "No, I suppose you have come here to have tea with me." replied Duscuth whose voice was heavy with sarcasm.

"No, more of a warning than tea, you see Zayal is going to be aiding the Orc army with his three bodyguards, I think you've met them, Lethe Eragor, Phlegethon McHale and Acheron Siphon, delightful little chi demons aren't they? Oh yes, you only defeated Ishvala cause I helped."

"What is this? You helped us beat Ishvala? You helped us? You know that I used to be the . . ." roared Duscuth but Seize cut him off "That is the point Duscuth 'you used to be', face it. You're a magical tramp now, Ishvala is the fastest Doomknight other than me. Your skeleton cavalry couldn't hit him, but I did. Bye bye old friend, good luck." He said with a smirk and disappeared.

Duscuth completely forgot about his audience with Odin and ran all the way back to the cabin and right onto the field. "Wow that was a sho— uh Duscuth you look like you have seen a ghost." commented Dravir "Not a ghost" he replied "but something even worse and three times as irritating . . ."

He told Dravir of what happened with Seize, but left out the fact that Seize had called him an old friend. "This is not good" said Hersuls "if Seize was telling the truth than we're in big trouble, there's probably only one other person here who has a decent chance of defeating Zayal and that's Odin."

"Zayal is more powerful than you think, he's the eighth Doomknight, when in this world his power is limited to forty percent, but if somehow he was able to bring us down to the underworld he could fight on par with Azruth." said Duscuth.

"Wait I thought Ishvala was the eighth. How is Zayal the eighth?" asked Dravir. "It's a long explanation but I'll tell you." replied Duscuth. "Do you know that Hyorin Katsura is a half demon?" Dravir and Hersuls nodded this was sounding interesting.

"He's also like you Dravir; half god, a son of Metistacia. Mietitore, the supposed ninth Doomknight, is only a half demon, not a drop of god blood in him. But he's got more control of that half demon soul, why I don't know. He uses the demon part of his soul to give him power, and when he releases that demon energy inside of him he's more powerful than Seize."

"So technically he's the first Doomknight?" asked Dravir "He can keep up that energy level for 3 days, so in order to kill him you need to do the deed before he releases full power, or else you'll be ripped to shreds." Duscuth said warily. "I wonder how you'll look in shredded form?" said Hersuls with dark humor.

At that very moment they heard a screeching sound echoing not too far from where they were. Duscuth jumped up and swore. "They've sent out scouts! Dravir, Hersuls get to the field and mount now!" he said the last word twice as loud as the others.

Dravir ran out followed by Hersuls. He mounted him and took off. Dravir Drew his sword. "Roar, Gehenam!"[hellfire] They flew for a few seconds without seeing any of the Orcs, but as soon as Dravir lowered his guard, a massive Orc tried to shoot him.

They were even more grotesque then what Duscuth had described. Their skin was a moldy green, and they gave out a horrible stench. Hersuls dove downward at it but was stopped in his tracks.

It was so fast Dravir barely had time to react, there was a blur of crimson and a flick of a sword, the Orc was cut in two. Dravir looked left and right but there was no one within a few hundred feet who could have done that.

"Alright Hersuls, no taking pity or getting afraid anymore, we'll have to fight." said Dravir. Hersuls nodded and flew towards the carnage. Twice more they met Orcs who left the front line to wreck havoc behind the backs of the Dwarves'.

The first time Hersuls bit it on the shoulder and slashed its' face with his claws. The next time Dravir shot the elf spell; *diplos fotia* [dual fires] at it, burning it up.

They flew passed a group of Dwarves fighting two Orcs and they reached the front lines. Then Dravir saw it again, crimson blur slashing the Orcs to pieces. "Hey!" shouted Hersuls "Quit looking at that. We need to get back in this fight."

Dravir turned away from the crimson blur and shot a wall of cursed flames at a nearby Orc. Several Orcs left their fights and charged at Hersuls and Dravir. '*Duscuth was right the Orcs did move fast.*' thought Dravir. They had managed to catch up to him in mere seconds. He slashed an Orc with his sword. Even more Orcs were charging towards them now and Dravir and Hersuls found themselves surrounded.

"We can't go on killing all of them, we'll be overwhelmed soon! shouted Hersuls. Dravir knew this was true, he had killed seven so far but they were still surrounded.

Dravir knew that there was no way out of this. "If we are going down, we'll take as many of them as we can with us." He shouted. Hersuls flew at the nearest Orc but stopped again. The crimson blur appeared and turned the surrounding Orcs into mincemeat. *'What the hell is that?'* thought Dravir. It was faster than anything he had ever seen. *'Wait, could it be Xephos Seize.'* Fear started to set in. They had barely been a match for Ishavala and Seize was supposed to be exponentially stronger.

"Let's find Duscuth!" shouted Hersuls. He dived straight into the battle field. There were only around seven Orcs left, probably just realizing that fact themselves they all turned and fled.

Dravir searched the crowd of cheering Dwarves for Duscuth, after some time he found him, sitting on a rope bridge away from the festivities. He was looking in the direction of the fleeing Orcs.

"How many will there be?" asked Hersuls. "Around six thousand." replied Duscuth. Dravir and Hersuls gaped. "Six thousand, we could barely handle the eighty that did this, and that crimson thing killed most of them." moaned Dravir. "True," said Duscuth, "But when they come next time, we will be waiting for them. Odin, his Iron Guard and the full wrath of the dwarves will be thrown at them."

Duscuth turned around. "Did you see it?" he asked. Dravir nodded. "Something tells me that wasn't a very complicated elf spell." muttered Hersuls. "My guess," Duscuth said, "is that Xephos Seize has been tampering again." "I thought just as much." Dravir said to general surprise. "So Orisis will arrest or execute him?"

"The chance of that happening is less than zero. Epta has too much power, it is the largest state in Drachen, and it has four Doomknights native to it. It contributes thirty percent of the entire army. Seize is a popular king, strangely. And Orisis doesn't want him as an enemy . . . for now."

CHAPTER 12

THE FIRST QUAD

Dravir walked with Hersuls and Duscuth to his cabin. When they got there they were mortified. There was an arrow in the lock, not a Dwarves' arrow the shaft was black and the spearhead and feathers were red.

Dravir unsheathed *Gehenam* [hellfire] and Duscuth took out *purustas ingel* [black angel] as well. Dravir silently crept towards the door, and Duscuth motioned that on the count of three to break it.

The first finger rose, the second finger rose, and finally the third finger rose. Dravir smashed through the door closely followed by Duscuth and Hersuls, to find a boy around his age lounging on a chair eating a tomato.

"Don't move!" said Dravir. The boy sighed, he had black hair, tan skin, he was tall and well built and had bandages wrapped around his arm and on his back there was a long and sleek bow.

"You moved!" said Dravir anger arising. "So breathing is illegal now, is it?" the boy shouted in reply. "Well yeah, it is." shouted Dravir. "No it's not!" the boy argued, he had a dangerous look in his eyes.

"What's your name?" asked Duscuth "Rivera, Ivan Rivera, son of Lazex, I know you people." Ivan said. Dravir, Hersuls and Duscuth looked astounded. "How do you-" asked Hersuls but he was cut off by Ivan. "I have been following you, just so I'm clear, you're Dravir, son of Morfos" he said pointing to Dravir "you're Duscuth, and the dragon/salamander hybrid is Hersuls."

"The dragon/salamander hybrid has ears you know" said Hersuls "And what makes you so sure that we'll trust you, son of Lazex." He was looking suspiciously at the stranger. "Because I have this." said Ivan he reached into his cloak and took out a parchment. He walked over to Duscuth and gave it to him. Duscuth read it and gave it back to him.

"Welcome to the team." he said. For the first time Ivan smiled but then almost immediately returned to his grim face.

"Wait, how can you just suddenly let him in?" asked Dravir and Hersuls in unison "That note" began Duscuth "was signed by the Third Elfish King and stated that he helped them get rid of a group of Shrukin's men and that he can be trusted. "The Elf King you say" said Dravir "well, if he thinks so and you do too, then I'll go with it." Hersuls nodded reluctantly.

"Right" said Duscuth "let's see if Lazex's talent with a bow has rubbed off on you." They got up and walked to the field. "Hersuls" said Duscuth "go ask Odin if-" but he was cut off by Ivan. "Don't worry about targets" he took out a flask out of his cloak, the liquid inside bore great resemblance to the liquid Ishvala used to try to kill them.

He drank it than touched the ground with both hands. Thirty, forty and fifty feet from where they were standing, fifteen archery targets erupted from the ground. "An archer and an alchemist, and by the looks of the targets, Imperial level, that is amazing!" exclaimed Duscuth. "He's just an endless amount of talent isn't he." Dravir muttered sarcastically.

Ivan took an arrow out of his quiver and shot each of the targets with speed and power. Duscuth went up to check his results. "Two bulls eyes, nine in the inner ring, and four in the second to inner ring." He shouted. "Truly impressive."

"Does Odin know you're here?" asked Hersuls. "No. Why ask?" replied Ivan. "How did you get inside the defenses?" he asked. "Same way Seize did, through the mountains" answered Ivan with a smile. "I saw him using shadow sprint to get up."

Duscuth nodded but Dravir asked "Shadow sprint?" Before Ivan could answer Duscuth explained "It's one of Seize's many techniques. He gives out lots of shadowy energy and pushes himself forward with it. Using it he'll be so fast you can't even see him, remember the blur, Seize was hardly using any effort."

"Then how'd you see it" asked Hersuls. "I didn't see him while using it" said Ivan getting slightly irritated "I saw him right before he was going to use it." Dravir nodded. "So why exactly are you helping us?" he asked "Your dealing with gods and immortality. I want that kind of power. Not to be a tyrant or anything, but to take back my home."

"And what would that be?" asked Duscuth "It's a small town in The Needles. It's called Lux." he answered Duscuth backed up and gasped. "That means you're a descendant of Anagmal!" said Duscuth. "And

THERE WILL BE WAR

you just lost me." said Hersuls. "Anagmal was an ancient kingdom, a city-state of sorts. Prosperous and peaceful. It was a mighty power and unmatched in almost every aspect. However a neighboring kingdom: Dunland, wanted to take the city. When they invaded, Anagmal inflicted a humiliating defeat on them. Dunland appealed for help. Thousands of soldiers came from other kingdoms. Anagmal was shortly burned to the ground. Only a few hundred of its people survived. A large portion settled in The Needles. Hence Lux was established." said Ivan

"If you are a descendant of this 'Anagmal' you should fight pretty well." said Dravir. "I do. However Lux is under occupation, by Orisis. He decimated its population and defiled my home." Ivan said. There was resentment in his eyes.

As they talked no one realized someone was walking toward them until they heard the persons' voice. "Sir, a few thousand or Orcs have been spotted by our scouts." It was a Dwarf. He noticed Ivan. "Hey, who're you?" he asked turning to the newest member of the group. "No time to explain." said Ivan already running towards the cabin.

"Well, I guess we should follow." said Dravir jumping on Hersuls. "Roar *Gehenam*![hellfire]. "I'm right behind you!" shouted Duscuth running behind Ivan.

Dravir and Hersuls flew at top speed to Odin's palace with Ivan and Duscuth not far behind. They landed in front of the gates, which were open. They rushed through; Odin was in full armor and had a giant battle axe in his hand.

He was talking to who Dravir believed were his generals. He moved two paces to the left and turned around to see where Duscuth was, to find Ivan flying straight into him.

"You idiot!" shouted Dravir, after he got back up. "Can't you even watch where you're going? I have half a mind to melt you with my sword!" Dravir drew his sword and pointed it threateningly at Ivan. "It's not my fault you oaf. If you hadn't moved at the last second I wouldn't have collided." Ivan shouted back.

Their shouting made Odin stop talking and turn towards them. He opened his mouth but then his eyes fell on Ivan. "Who the bloody hell are you!?!" he boomed. The arguing stopped. Ivan turned towards Odin and handed him the note.

"Elves, they are scheming creatures. I've got a good mind not to listen to this rubbish." Thankfully Duscuth had just arrived at that minute. "Lord Odin," he said "I trust this boy and you should too, he's dealt decent cards to Shrukin himself." Odin surveyed Ivan. It seemed as if he was looking for something. In the end he relented. "Very well, because you trust him so shall I. But now is not the time for bickering among yourselves, we have a war to fight!"

CHAPTER 13

THE FALLEN HERO

Odin and his Iron Guard accompanied them to the front lines. The Iron Guard that pretty much described its members. Their armor, helmets, weapons and all other war necessities were all made of iron.

Dravir could see the war tents ahead with their blue and silver flags flying high. Their primary banner however, was a silver battleaxe on a blue field. Dravir was nervous and by the looks of it so was Hersuls, but strangely not Ivan. He was standing still looking dignified. *'He is totally outclassing me. I can't let that happen.'* thought Dravir.

Dravir picked up his pace. He strode in front of Ivan. The son of Lazex, in turn increased his pace. This contest of egos continued till Duscuth yelled at the two of them. Odin turned around, looking stern. The entire company went silent.

Just then Tyr ran toward them. With him were couple other dwarves who were looking worn out. "Eragor, McHale and Siphon spotted with Zayal Doncanson!" he gasped.

Dravir's confidence slightly improved. "You beat them last time, why should you be worried?" asked Dravir. "We didn't beat them, we surprised them with some lucky shots and made it improbable for them to kill you." replied Tyr. Dravir's newfound confidence evaporated.

"Duscuth and I will deal with them." said Ivan. Tyr opened his mouth to ask who he was but looking at Duscuth's face he realized this was not the time. "I'm going to speak with Odin about tactics." said Duscuth and walked away. Then they heard the screeching again.

"It's time to go to war." said Dravir.

There was a wave of green two hundred feet ahead of them. "Let's go!" said Hersuls. And the three charged along with eight thousand Dwarves *"Sacer ingnis murum!"* [wall of cursed fire] shouted Dravir. The green flames consumed two Orcs. The battle was ragging on and on. Orcs screeched against the Dwarfish battle cries. The fighters on either side were being slashed and sliced.

Dravir was in fighting mode. Hack slash dodge parry! His mind was going a mile a minute. He skewered an incoming Orc. Three more charged to take its place. Slash cut thrust deflect flick. Dravir dispatched the Orcs.

He turned to see how Ivan and Hersuls were doing. Ivan and Hersuls were doing quite well. Ivan was shooting down Orcs, left right and center. He was providing the dwarves with long range support. Hersuls flew over the ranks of Orcs, harassing them. However the Dwarves were not doing so well.

They were scattered and not fighting well. The Orcs out maneuvered them and crippled them with poison breath. Dwarves were falling everywhere. But then a giant voice boomed "Men, stand your ground, do not let them take a single step towards our soil, you must fight!" It was Odin and the Iron Guard. They flung themselves on the enemy crushing everything in their paths.

The other Dwarves, inspired by this, started fighting even harder. Then something caught Dravir's eye. Duscuth had used elf spell 29 *dynami pido*,[power jump] to land in enemy lines. "Materialize *purustas ingel*!" he heard him say.

"Ivan, Hersuls to me!" shouted Dravir. Hersuls flew down to him with Ivan tailing. "We need to get far into enemy lines, Duscuth's alone there!" said Dravir as he slashed an Orc. Ivan and Dravir jumped on Hersuls and flew. They took off into the sky and flew twenty feet. Then Hersuls stopped dead.

Then they saw it, Zayal Doncanson, Lethe Eragor, Phlegethon McHale and Acheron Siphon had each stabbed Duscuth in the stomach. The world had ended, but the battle raged onward. One by one they took their swords out, first Doncanson, then Eragor, then Siphon and finally McHale.

There were smirks on all of their faces, and the nearest Orcs let out a wave of cheers. "NOOOOOOO!!!!!" howled Dravir "I'm going to kill you Doncanson!" He jumped of Hersuls, "*Sacer ingnis murum*" [wall of cursed fire] he screamed. Doncanson looked up smiling. He pointed upward with one finger shot a blast of red light straight at Dravir.

Dravir easily parried, he flicked his sword in a deadly arc and changing the direction of the blast. Thud! Dravir landed on the ground,

Eragor, Siphon and McHale lunged at him but were stopped by half a dozen arrows. Ivan and Hersuls landed next to him.

"We'll keep the chi demons busy, you deal with Doncanson." shouted Ivan. Dravir ran toward him. Zayal stood calmly ahead and quietly unsheathed an odd looking sword. Clang! The two swords met. "So this is the new Facce Pax, eh, Katsura was right you are a weakling." He said with a sneer. The Doomknight moved his sword so fast that Dravir barely had time to react.

Doncanson was easily a better swordsman than he was. Performing complex attacks with ease. He sliced and cut with speed, power and was rarely off balance. Doncanson didn't even bother looking at his fight. Instead he looked at the battle and Odin crushing Orcs. "It's over," he said "I killed one member of the quad; the prophecy will never be fulfilled."

Dravir had no idea what in hell he was talking about, but it just made him angrier. Slashing with full power and hatred in every stroke, these very strokes would have terrified any standard warrior, but they didn't break Doncanson's defense. There was a sound at the back of his head, it sounded like Blaze's maniacal laughter.

"Well I best take leave now. Boy, you can have this." he said as Dravir slashed. He conjured a parchment out of thin air. Dravir brought his sword up, but Doncanson had vanished. He turned around, the three chi demon and the Orcs had also vanished into thin air.

"Damn it! Doncanson come back you bastard and fight me . . . !" "It's over Dravir." said Ivan holding him back. Dravir was shaking with anger. "It. Is. Not. Over!" Dravir shouted through clenched teeth "That bastard stabbed Duscuth."

"Oh god, Duscuth!" Ivan and Dravir turned around.

Ivan and Dravir ran towards the body to find Hersuls already over there. He was the first to speak; "Duscuth we can get you to the-", but Duscuth stopped him, blood came out of his mouth along with a few coughs as he spoke his last words. "Six years ago, I was the sixth Doomknight." And then his eyes slid out of focus and he met oblivion.

Dravir could not believe it. Duscuth was dead. It was impossible and yet in this battle it was true. Xephos Seize had not helped them this time. Tears rolled down his cheek and through blurred vision he saw Hersuls crying as well.

"Great gods of gold!" Dravir heard someone gasp. He looked up; it was Odin, Tyr and some other Dwarves. There was a long, gloomy and desolate silence. "What happened?" asked Tyr finally breaking it.

"Doncanson stabbed him, Eragor, Siphon and McHale too." croaked Dravir.

"The battlefield is his grave," said Ivan "we should honor that." He took out an arrow out of his quiver and shot it down, and then he shot another, and another, until there was a bed of arrows.

Odin and Tyr picked up his body and laid it on the bed. Then Hersuls close his eyes and slowly spat some fire out. The fire took the form on a majestic dome large enough to accommodate the bed of arrows. The dome then collapsed, and Duscuth disappeared forever.

Dravir slowly walked towards the piece of parchment that Zayal dropped. He picked it up and read it, it was a prophecy, the same prophecy that Lazex had narrated to Orisis.

> 'A quad of fighters shall seek and slay
> One through nine they will make pay
> The lost ones shall be brought back
> Though two will have souls to lack
> The power of fear will be tested
> Or else be evenly bested
> Morfos' child shall grow great
> But in his power is not his fate
> If his good heart fails to win
> Then he will be doing many a sin
> The Black King will stand and fight
> For the mortal throne is his right'

Well this is a waste of time thought Dravir miserably; Duscuth's gone, so there will never be a quad, Orisis wins. He closed his eyes. Standing in front of him was Blaze. "You're not going to let trash like Orisis make you give up, are you?"

Blaze was right, Dravir knew it. He opened his eyes. "So," said Ivan "what's our next move?" "We move to the Ormis Baymis." said Dravir, "I've got a score to settle."

DEATH KNIGHTS ARC

CHAPTER 14

SHADOW FIST

It was a dark night. Orisis stood alone, inside a large black room. On the wall behind him was a silver sword going through a skull; the crest of the Death Knights. Diagonally behind him to his left was a red gong.

Next to the Doomknights the thirty Death Knights were the most feared and powerful. Becoming a Death Knight granted you 'lord' status. They were sent on tasks that required immediate attention, like crushing an open rebellion and assassination or annihilation.

The thirty were divided into seven teams of four people. Plus two single units, the commander and the second in command. Each team was known as a circle. With the first circle being the most powerful and the seventh circle; the least, the commander and second in command being circle zero.

There was a knock on the door. "Come in." Orisis said, his voice boomed through the room. Hyorin Katsura walked in. "Sound the call of darkness." commanded Orisis. Hyorin Katsura obeyed, he hit the gong with his fist.

Several black forms appeared in the room bowing to Orisis. "Ah, Death Knights, how long it's been. I have a new mission for you. It is something that will require your immediate attention. An assassination mission, it should be done quickly. Your targets are Dravir Xeres, Ivan Rivera and Hersuls the Knaves. Leave no evidence that you were there."

The Death Knights bowed their head. "Yes master." Came cold whispers. Then they disappeared.

"Hyorin Katsura, you could learn manners from these boys." said Orisis as he left the room. "When Skrall sends a person back from hell." He replied after Orisis was out of the room.

*   *   *

Dravir, Ivan and Hersuls had left the Dwarves, after a lavish feast in honor of the dwarves' victory and Duscuth's official funeral. As they left, Tyr caught up to them. "You sure you're going?" he asked. "We've all agreed that since Duscuth, well expired, Dravir is going to make the decisions." said Ivan.

"Well take this." said Tyr He reached into his armor and took out a bag full of coins. "Dravir you're going to want to see this." said Ivan. Dravir turned around and gasped. Tyr nodded. Dravir took the bag. "May we meet again someday." shouted Tyr as they walked away from Aminas.

"Dravir, why are we going to the Ormis Baymis?" asked Hersuls. "We will get help there. We can meet up with allies, people who will help us." Ivan found a small flaw in this plan "So where exactly do we go?" asked Ivan. Dravir opened his mouth to answer but then closed it. "I don't know."

After traveling for two days, the company landed in an endless woodland. In simple words; they were lost. "We're lost!" moaned Hersuls. "No we are not, I think we are on the right path!" shouted Dravir. The stress of leading a group on his own was getting to him; he wondered how Duscuth had done it.

"Look!" said Ivan suddenly "Over there, there's a small house." Hersuls and Dravir turned towards it almost immediately. There, fifty feet toward their right was a house. But something was wrong. All the trees around the house were dead despite the fact that it was late spring.

Dravir looked at Ivan. "So the trees are dead, so what?" he asked. Hersuls looked at Dravir expectantly. "Fine then, we go." Dravir said. They walked towards the house, but stopped.

Ivan tapped Dravir's shoulder. "Death Knights," He whispered, "They're hiding up in the trees. Four or five of them, though I don't know which circle they are from."

"What?" asked Dravir, not comprehending. But then there were bangs all around them. Four cloaked figures had appeared around them. "There's a Knaves with them, they must be the ones." One of them hissed.

"Then we fight," said the one on his left. "Take of your cloaks, we must give our targets the honor of realizing who we are." With that each of the cloaked figures ripped of their cloaks. Each one wore something different, each one was more fearsome than the last.

The one who had spoken first wore a blood red robe and held a red staff with a skull on the top with his right hand. He had a skull mask that covered only half his face. The visible half of his face was well groomed and had red hair. He had a long white scar on his left arm, the same arm which he had long black claws.

The one to his left wore black armor trimmed gold and a helmet that looked like a bat's head with a slit where its eyes should be. Only his eyes were visible, and he wielded a scythe. His left arm was not a human arm, it was rough and green. His arm wasn't the strangest thing about him, when Dravir looked at him, his Iris and Pupil turned purple and the rest of his eye turned black.

The one to his left wore only the black, what looked like dragon scale pants and had the Death Knight's mark tattooed on his chest, he was monstrously tall, slung on his back was the longest and thickest blade Dravir had ever seen. He had long black hair covering one of his eyes. His left arm was massive, pumped with muscles, and it was copper in color.

The last member was also wearing armor, but his was normal, other than the fact that there was no metal sleeve for his left arm. That arm was grey and had a red line running down till his hand till it broke into five lines going to each finger. That arm must have been metal because in his left hand he held an immensely large and spiky battle mace's top.

"My apologies," said the one wearing the red robe, "we haven't introduced our selves we are Shadow fist. I'm Antonius, Fire mage of the seventh circle." The man with the bat mask spoke "I am Mortem, Scythe master, belonging to the seventh circle." The giant man with the pumped hand spoke next. "I am Eras, seventh circles' master of the iron blade." "And I" said the last man "am Leiche, steel alchemist of the seventh circle."

"Right," said Dravir "I'm Dravir Xeres Facce Pax of the . . . um, uh twelfth circle." The Death Knights looked at themselves. Then Eras drew his sword, it was bigger than it seemed when slung on his back. "Right, I hope you go easy on me." he said sarcastically.

He charged a blinding speed and slashed. *Gehenam* and the other sword clashed in midair. Boom! The stroke alone sent Dravir flying back. "That's it? That's the power of the legendry last rider of the Knaves." gloated Eras. "*Sacer ingnis murum!*" [wall of cursed fire] shouted Dravir. Eras easily deflected with his hand.

Ivan drew an arrow to shoot him. "Oh no Lux boy, I'm your opponent." said Leiche. He flicked his arm and it sprouted a sword out of his hand. He dropped the mace top. Ivan shot an arrow as a test.

His arrow was deflected by a large metal shield that manifested out of thin air. It then disappeared again.

He swore under his breath. He shot another arrow. Again a metal shield blocked it. "Damn you Leiche, give me an accursed opening." The alchemist was not breaking a sweat.

Hersuls ran towards Dravir while Ivan shot arrows at Leiche. But Mortem appeared in front of him. "No helping him, I'm going to send you to hell!" he shouted.

As he attacked the landscape tore and terror spread. Each stroke was performed with incredible precision. It was exceedingly tough for Hersuls to dodge them. "So that's why you're supposedly a scythe master." he muttered.

The fights raged on. Antonius, however remained stationary and observed. It was clear that the Dravir, Ivan and Hersuls were outmatched. Antonius smiled. He had waited for such a moment his entire career. He would be a great hero in the eyes of Orisis.

"Don't you get it, without Duscuth you're all hopelessly out matched." He shouted with glee. "You're all going to die, and we will bring your bodies to Lord Orisis and be honored above even the Doomknights."

Dravir glanced at the other fights, it was true, and their chances of victory were thinner than they'd ever be while Duscuth was still around. '*Oh gods, how did I get us into such a terrible mess.*' thought Dravir as he readied himself for another attack on Eras.

CHAPTER 15

THE GIRL WITH THE GREEN HAIR

The battle raged on. Dravir was getting pummeled by Eras. Ivan was fighting a long lost battle against Leiche and Hersuls could only fly away as Mortem used his scythe. In short, they were in a bit of a pickle.

"Eat my blade!" shouted Dravir charging at Eras. "I think I will." He replied. He stepped backward, bent down and bit the blade. "That was not literal." said Dravir shuddering. Eras spat out the blade and punched Dravir in the stomach. "You'll need a miracle or magic to win." He shouted.

'Magic, why did I not think about magic?' thought Dravir. He stood up and used the most powerful spell he knew. "*Demonio hechizo cuarenta y cinco rugido de fuego!*" [Demon spell forty five roar of fire] A blazing red large inferno shot out of Dravir's hands towards Eras and collided with a boom. Eras flew back and collided with the house.

It was not what Dravir expected. Eras lay unconscious in the tavern. "Right," he said, "One down three to go. You're next Antonius!" he charged. Antonius' staff melted into a black silk glove with a navy blue circle on it. "Midnight inferno!" he shouted. He slashed the air with his hand. A large blast of fire shot out of Antonius' hand and sped towards Dravir.

"What the hell?" shouted Dravir as he jumped out of the way. "This is a special fire. It's not as explosive or durable as normal fire, but it burns two hundred times better." said Antonius with another slash and midnight fire. "It's time to stop holding back and finish this fight."

Meanwhile Leiche and Mortem were starting to wrap up their fights, "Enough of this," spat Leiche "Time for me to use my famous iron arm." He flicked his arm and it became a two foot long metal spike, with that he charged.

Mortem stopped swinging his scythe around Hersuls. He pointed his left arm at Hersuls, who was flying thirty feet away. The arm increased until it was twenty feet long. Then the fore most eighteen feet started morphing.

After twenty seconds the ex-arm was a fifteen foot tall and eight foot wide double door with images of monsters on it. "Gate of the all consuming Hellhound I open thee!" shouted Mortem.

The double doors parted and a blood red, two headed dog with a twelve foot long scorpion tail, the size of the rock of Aminas emerged. "Dear god." is all what Hersuls managed to say.

The Hellhound roared, the roar shook the Earth itself, and was about to open its mouth to consume Hersuls when there was a flash of light at the monster's throat and its head came off. All the fighting stopped, even the Death Knights stopped to look.

The flash of light had taken a humanoid shape holding a sword. The thing charged towards Mortem at speeds inhuman and cut of the gate-hand. Mortem howled with pain and drew his sword to challenge the usurper.

Sparks flew as the two swords clashed, Dravir got over his shock of the 'light' and found an opening to slash Antonius. Silently he drew closer and closer till he was in range. Then, he slashed. Blood spewed and flew out as Dravir slashed Antonius' back.

Antonius turned back. "Not . . . possible . . ." he croaked as he fell to the ground, unconscious. Dravir turned back toward the fight, Mortem had been defeated with the combined help of Ivan and the 'light'. And now they were engaging Leiche.

Realizing that all his allies had been defeated, he jumped back and dissolved into the shadows, along with the bodies of Antonius, Eras and Mortem. "Run away like cowards." muttered Ivan.

But then the three of them turned towards the 'light'. "Who, in the name of Bravec are you?" asked Hersuls. "Well," it said "I am who I am, but considering you asked me and want an adequate answer . . ." This was the kind of answer that pissed Ivan off. "Just shut up and tell us who you are!" he roared.

"I am Celandia Hoffnung, daughter of Dominus Hoffnung, Commander of the Ormis Baymis." it said. Then there was an explosion of gold light for a split second and the light had gone, and it its place stood a girl with green hair.

THERE WILL BE WAR

She was almost as tall as Dravir, she had brown eyes, and she wore sleeveless armor with an omega symbol in the center [Ω] and a red skirt. Her green hair came down to her waist.

"So I hear you lot are looking for the Ormis Baymis." asked Celandia. "Who wants to kn-" said Hersuls. But he was cut off by Dravir "Right you are!" "Well then you found your way." She said. "Follow me; it's a long walk that'll take eighteen days."

"Well then, you've never flown before!" said Dravir as he mounted Hersuls. "Come on." He said to Celandia, who was looking nervous. "I'm not sure, can you support that much weight?" she asked, looking at Hersuls. "Rest assured," the Knaves said "I can carry almost twice this weight."

Dravir showed the two newer members how to mount. They learned quickly and got it in one try. When all three people were on, Hersuls took off. As he rose, he grunted. Dravir looked as if he was going to say something, but was cut off by Hersuls. "I'm fine. Don't worry about me."

CHAPTER 16

THE HUNT FOR THE LAST SHARD

"So Mortem, Leiche, Eras and Antonius, team Shadow fist, you failed your mission. You engaged your targets, but you lost." said a voice lurking in the shadows of Shadow fist's headquarters. "Well that mission is insignificant compared to what I'm going to send you on."

The figure emerged, he was tall, elegant and yet vicious and vindictive. He wore simple black battle armor with no helmet and a black silk cape. His face was flickering, sometimes a man of twenty eight, sometimes a plain white skull.

He picked up a scroll and gave it to Leiche. The Deathknight read it. He was stunned. "Lord Shadoe," He began "surely you are not thinking of . . ." "Yes I am," Shadoe interrupted "I will bring back the two fallen ones and turn them against their brother. Then this new group of 'heroes' will feel the full power of the Fifth Doomknight."

"You are rightly named 'Wrath' the most heartless of the nine." said Leiche. Shadoe frowned. He wasn't fond of flattery. "Flattery will get you nowhere Leiche. Croxeth is disappointed with your results." The last sentence sent a shiver down the backs of the Death Knights. Croxeth, was the head of the Death Knights. There was a rumor that he was offered a position in the Doomknights.

Leiche swallowed uncertainly. However Shadoe's expression changed. He looked strangely content. "Yet, you managed to give us more information than Hyorin Katsura."

"Your instructions are clear Shadow fist," The necromancer looked down on the Death Knights. Like a lion looking a mouse. "Find the pieces. The city's governor already has most of it. There is only one piece left from each. Find it or suffer the consequences." said Shadoe. He turned around and erupted in a pillar of fire.

Only when they were sure he was gone did the Death Knights speak. "Oh sure," said Mortem, "he gets to erupt in fire, but we get to hunt for some stupid egg." He looked around. All his fellows were looking angry. This was menial work for people of their status.

"A stupid egg is it, Mortem? Something that came from one of those stupid eggs nearly killed the chi demon McHale." A voice from the shadows spoke. The four turned toward the direction of the voice.

A figure emerged. He had wild and spiky yellow hair and a vicious grin. The man wore a black shirt, bronze pants and had bronze cape with a bolt of lightning going through a skull imprinted on it. And etched on the back of his hand in blood was the Death knight crest.

"Oh, Naxos, it's just you." said Antonius. That pissed Naxos off. He was speaking to insects, and they had the gall to insult him "Shut your mouth insect! I am the second in command of the Death Knights. I could crush you like the maggot you are." Naxos took a deep breath. He had been instructed personally by Orisis not to fry any more Death Knights. Though he despised having to control his rage, orders were orders. His focus returned to the seventh circle. "Croxeth wanted me to tell you that he already found one piece. Your task has been simplified. All you have to do, is find the last one and mend them."

"The Commander was looking for egg pieces?" asked Eras. Naxos glared at them. He desperately wanted to fry them. "Alright, alright we're going, we're going." said Antonius. The four left the building and dissolved into the breeze.

*　　*　　*

"I hate using 'shadow mist'." grumbled Eras. "It gives me motion sickness." His three companions found this statement to be quite odd. "Shut up, it is the only way to go three thousand miles without walking." snapped Antonius. They were in Ilrea. This was where Xephos Seize had found Duscuth. The Death Knights looked around. Here they had no superiors. That was a pleasant thought and their usual swagger and arrogance returned.

A troop of men approached them. Mortem smiled. He enjoyed scaring the common men. The captain walked up towards them. "Sir," he said to Antonius. "Lord Croxeth has instructed us to show you where the traitor Duscuth lived." Antonius saw his chance. He like most Death Knights had a colossal ego. He believed that it was his birthright to lord over lesser soldiers. "Do it." he spat. The captain nervously backed up and turned around and led the way.

"I wonder how Croxeth couldn't find the second piece. He is rumored to be as powerful as Cyphrure." muttered Mortem loud enough so that only Antonius could hear. "It's a simple spell, that too." As the people looking out of their window withdrew immediately and patrols snapped to attention.

"Ah, it's nice to be respected and feared again." sighed Eras, basking in the mix of fear and respect of the people. The group navigated themselves to a poorer part of Ilrea. They weaved through alleys and shacks. The troop suddenly stopped. "Sir," shouted the captain "we have arrived." Antonius walked forward, on the ground he drew seven circles. Then pointing to each respectively he said "Arrive ye shard and appease thy master."

"Like I said, it was a simple retrieval spell." said Mortem. With a burst of light an eighth circle appeared. "Appeal to the Air God" a voice cackled "Disectas una Bravec, Disectas una Bravec!" chanted Antonius.

Then the eighth circle disappeared. "I-It didn't work?" stammered the captain wondering what kind of black magic this was. "Not really," said Antonius turning around "I know exactly where it is."

"Right then, let's go get the egg." spat Mortem. The company followed Antonius. "I believe the last piece is under the dirt." He said. He looked downward and searched it for anything sticking out.

Suddenly he bent down. "I found it." He muttered. Mortem, seeing it to, picked up the last piece and handed it to Eras. He tore the sleeve of his green arm off.

Tattooed on his arm, was the Death Knight logo. He pressed it with his other arm. Ten feet in front of them Naxos materialized. "Well well, Shadow fist you pulled through. I was cynical, but it seems I was wrong." Naxos' ever-present scowl broke for a second. "I'll be taking that then." He said, grabbing the piece. "Cruel blackguard!" shouted Mortem, drawing his sword.

Naxos' scowl returned. "At any rate, Lord Shadoe will be pleased. Now we can continue our plan to resurrect the other two Knaves!"

GOD THEORY ARC

CHAPTER 17

MIDNIGHT EYE

Hersuls, Dravir, Ivan, and Celandia were flying without a single idea about the horrors that Edmund Shadoe was cooking up. "Are we there yet?" asked Hersuls. "I've heard people being transported saying that. This, however, is the first time I've heard the transporter say that." chuckled Dravir.

"So Celandia, what was that light distortion thing you were doing?" asked Ivan. "That's my magic: Rytstar, it allows me to change into seven differently elemental armors. The one you saw was light or Snet Neves." "Interesting" remarked Dravir. It was the first bit of magic he had seen that wasn't an Elf or Demon spell.

"Judging by Hersuls' speed it will be at least four hours before we reach. Do you want to land Hersuls?" asked Celandia. "Anytime." groaned Hersuls as he flew towards the ground. They landed in a clearing, that Celandia said was in northern Erete.

The group dismounted Hersuls relaxed. Despite what he had said, carrying three people was strenuous. Dravir noticed Celandia looking at some trees. He approached her. "Don't move." she breathed. Dravir, Hersuls and Ivan froze. "Someone is around here, somewhere, I feel a powerful presence." she whispered.

"Black crack, open!" A voice crackled out of nowhere. Then at the edge of the clearing a black portal door appeared, and Xephos Seize stepped out. "Oh, great god Ocathacaru, that makes my body numb. I'll be with you in one second."

The three stared at each other. Great, thought Dravir of all the Doomknights we get the odd one. After a couple of seconds Xephos Seize said "Dravir, Hersuls, Ivan and Celandia, I am Xephos Seize, bane of Altolen." Of course this introduction was unnecessary; they all knew who Seize was. Celandia drew her sword.

Seize looked at her. The scary thing was, there was nothing to suggest Seize was going to fight her. He was looking amused. "Come now," the Doomknight said. "Put that thing away. People will begin to think you are seriously trying to fight me." Seize laughed, as if the idea was completely unthinkable.

Dravir's attention turned to Seize's sword. The King of Epta had an odd looking blade with him. It was abnormally thin but very long, at least four feet. Its hilt was grey, its guard glowed orange and it had a long fang attached to the bottom of the hilt. *'How would you fight with something like that?'* thought Dravir.

Seize must have realized he was looking at it. "This is *Shini Kage* it's my blade, like *Gehenam* is yours. Anyway, if you want to talk about weapons, you will have to approach me later." Seize winked. "I've come to warn Hersuls, Sir Edmund Shadoe, is going to bring back the other two. His castle is in South Erete, and it would be disastrous if he got away with it. I know it isn't my business but I really would do something about it."

"Hold on," said Dravir "why are you helping us. You were there in Animas. You were there when we fought Ishvala, and now you are here. Am I supposed this is from the goodness of your heart? I want an explanation!"

Seize smiled, as if he was expecting this. The Doomknight was silent for a few minutes. Dravir pressed his advantage. "See, you don't have an answer." Seize opened his mouth. "I have a question. How did you see me reacting to that in your head? It is quite curious."

Dravir was at a loss for words. He had absolutely no idea what was going on. "Furthermore," Seize continued. Ivan groaned. "I object to this line of questioning. My motives are my own. They will be revealed only when I chose to reveal them." Seize spoke the last sentence with such force that Dravir backed up.

"I have another piece of information." Seize said. "And . . . ?" Celandia prompted, after Seize spoke. "'And' what?" Seize asked "Who says I was going to reveal it." Dravir hit his head with frustration. *'Doesn't he have something more important to do?'* he wondered.

"But . . ." Seize said Dravir looked up. He was tired of this nonsense. "I like you people. You are my favorite threat to Orisis. So I have decided to tell you." *'What the hell is wrong with this man.'* Dravir wondered. He had imagined an encounter with Xephos Seize, but it went nothing like this. "There is a new Doomknight." Seize said. "*What?*" The group shouted in unison. Seize nodded. "His name is Iaeptus Omerta, he is quite a lout don't you think so?" Dravir was infuriated. He wanted to kill this man; there was just something so annoying about him. "Okay, I think you have helped us enough. We are going to go now." He said. He turned around to mount Hersuls.

"Stop, I am not sure that you understand me."

Seize now sounded completely serious. The hint of amusement and whimsy that he had previously spoken with vanished. "It is a high risk scenario. You *have* to stop Shadoe. It is not an option. Have I been understood?" Dravir nodded his head, Seize radiated power, the likes of which he had never seen. "Good." The Doomknight said.

Xephos Seize snapped his fingers and he disappeared into the wind.

Finally after a minute of two of silence, Ivan broke it. "Hersuls what was Seize talking about? What is Edmund Shadoe doing?" Hersuls had been oddly quiet during the encounter. He now looked sad and deeply disturbed. "There were three eggs" moaned Hersuls, "The other two were destroyed. I survived. Shadoe plans to resurrect the other two."

Dravir, Ivan and Celandia's faces lost all the color they had gained since Xephos Seize left. "How though?" asked Celandia "It is common knowledge that you need a body to resurrect something. How would it be possible to resurrect them?"

"Fragmented pieces of their eggs" croaked Hersuls. "He'll use the broken egg. We have got to stop this. The Ormis Baymis can wait." Strangely it was Celandia that spoke. "Definitely, we need to stop this. If Edmund Shadoe has two undead Knaves, getting you there safely won't matter.

"Then it's decided!" said Ivan "We attack the shadowy castle, or whatever it's called." "It is actually called 'The dark mountain'. The people who live nearby fear the castle. They say that people are experimented on. The castle of itself is monstrous. Its walls are massive, and it is strategically well placed." said Celandia.

"Do you know anymore about the castle?" asked Ivan slightly sarcastically. "No, that is about it." replied Celandia. Dravir was thinking. Breaking and entering into a Doomknight's castle would be suicide, if they were caught. But Celandia and Hersuls were of the opinion that Shadoe having undead Knaves would be just as risky. It was a tough call. He looked at Hersuls. The Knaves was in deep pain.

Dravir made his call. "What are you lot sitting around for? We got ourselves castle to raid." said Dravir as he mounted his Knaves. Hersuls' face lit up.

"So does anyone know anything about Shadoe, other than the fact that he is the fifth Doomknight?" Dravir asked when they were up in the air. "Nope" said Ivan. "Nothing." said Hersuls.

"Yes" said Celandia. Ivan and Dravir turned towards her. "He is supposedly more powerful than the fifth circle Death Knights combined. He is also supposed to be the greatest necromancer in the world" "Wonderful," muttered Ivan, "lots of *Leiches*."

"The other two looked at him. "Leaches?" asked Dravir. "Leiches, not Leaches. said Ivan, chuckling. "Oh Leiches." said Dravir starting to laugh. "I do not get it?" said Celandia. Dravir looked at her, then realized that she really didn't. "The man Ivan was fighting before you came, his name is Leiche." said Dravir between laughs.

"Oh . . ." said Celandia, "I still don't get it." Dravir and Ivan laughed again. They were flying above a valley at the time. It wasn't an ugly scene but it definitely was not picturesque. "This is perhaps the most foreboding journey I have ever undertaken." Ivan said "Well, unless we are attacked by someone, I would hardly call this a journey." declared Hersuls. "Don't jinx it." muttered Dravir.

Speak of the devil. The cloud they were about to fly into solidified and Hersuls hit it with a smack. "See, what did I tell you." Dravir said, dazed and dizzy. Then they fell. "Hersuls you flying string bean, get us out of this, I don't want to be a spot in the middle of nowhere.

Then just like the cloud, the air under them solidified two feet before they hit the ground. They were in a dark clearing with huge and ancient trees all around. "Please tell me this is an elf spell." said Ivan looking at Dravir. Dravir shook his head. Ivan gulped, "I think we are going to meet a couple of Death Knights, stronger than circle seven"

The four got up, and the air returned to normal and they fell down with a thud. "Man, Lord Bravec isn't happy today, what in hell did we do to offend him." muttered Ivan. "Lord Bravec did not do that," said Celandia, "we are dealing with a sorcerer of the air."

"What do you think Grimoire? How long will it take for us to beat them." someone said, lurking behind the trees. The voice was like the roar of fire. "I don't know. Why don't you ask Atmos, he's the one who got them here." came a gruff voice behind yet another tree, supposedly belonging to 'Grimoire'. "Don't ask me Drakkon, you know I don't like dealing with menial nonsense." Another voice spoke from in the trees. The voice was airy and heavily sarcastic.

"Well then let me do this myself, if they could beat Shadow fist, then maybe they qualify for trash." said the man called Drakkon. "Show yourselves!" shouted Celandia. "Oh, but if the lady wants, we will show ourselves." Came the airy voice of Atmos.

Dravir turned to Ivan "Get . . ." Ivan was trembling. "T-the m-man t-that—led th-he attack on L-Lux, w-was called Dr—Dra—Drakkon." His eyes were full of terror. "My my, could this be the encounter I've been waiting for. Ivan Rivera, how nice to see you again." said Drakkon, his voice full of glee. "I remember you. When we took Lux in the name of Orisis you ran away like a frightened child. It was pathetic." Drakkon began to laugh.

Celandia lost her temper, she shouted towards the source of the voices "IF YOU DON'T COME OUT, I'LL ACTIVATE RYTSTAR AND FIND YOU!!!" Laughter echoed throughout the woods. "Well you are an impatient one. Your wish is Midnight eye's command." came Grimoire's voice. "It is time to fight. But please forgive us if you lose several appendages . . . or your puny lives, Drakkon, you first."

"So it begins . . ." Drakkon said ominously.

CHAPTER 18

DRAKKON, GRIMOIRE AND ATMOS

"Damn these Death Knights, they always have to make things complicated, don't they." muttered Dravir. "Um, Dravir, I know this isn't a good time, but look behind you." Celandia said. Dravir turned around. What he saw gave him the bizarre feeling of wanting to laugh and run away screaming at the same time.

There was a man with dark brown hair pulled back showing his forehead. His eyes were slanting making him look like a typical villain. He wore a black shirt and wine red pants. His appearance wasn't the strangest thing about him though. He was standing on the back of a hovering twelve foot pure white King cobra with red eyes and massive fangs.

"You're standing on a snake." was all Dravir managed before he started laughing nervously. Drakkon's nostril's flared. Dravir had managed to anger him. "Yes I am. Why don't you try and hit me with that nice looking sword of yours." He spat back. It was Celandia that answered the challenge. "Rytstar, activate, holy armor of the golden light: Snet Neves."

As expected the golden light wrapped around her body and she charged at Drakkon with the amazing speed that armor granted. Surprisingly even with the speed she had, every attack missed its target. Celandia fell back, panting. The Death Knight weaved in and out, dodging ever one of Celandia's strokes.

Drakkon looked at her "Is that it? Maybe you are not worth our time or effort." Celandia glared at him, then shouted "Maybe this will be more to your liking. I will crush you! Heavens shake and feel the power of fire: Pozham titania!"

A pillar of fire covered her and when it disappeared all that remained was a humanoid shape covered with ash and fire. Celandia charged and yet again every attacked did not come close to hitting its target. Drakkon's snake was surprisingly agile. It moved away from Celandia at every opportunity. It threw her off balance several times.

"You are pathetic and puny. This fight bores me. Don't even bother trying; you stand no chance against me. Go fight Grimoire, maybe he will be closer to your speed." It was more of a mockery than a suggestion. As soon as he said it he turned pure white for a split second and then vanished.

The man called Grimoire came out from behind the trees. If there was a person who looked exactly like Skrall, it would be him. He was an exact replica of the Lord of the underworld except for the fact that there was a visible head under his hood.

He stood right in front of a tree making his shadow extremely long and wide. "What's he doing? Why isn't he attacking?" asked Hersuls. Realization dawned on Dravir "Look at his shadow." He whispered, terrified.

Out of the Death Knight's shadow came the shadows of Hellhounds, Giants Trolls, Orcs, and dead and decayed human beings. The shadows spread to other trees and suddenly looked toward the group of four.

Then they walked or slithered or moved however they did towards them. Then like magic, for every shadow a monster appeared. "Morfos save us." muttered Dravir before drawing *Gehenam*. But at the last second, Grimoire called a halt. The monsters froze. He looked up at the group. "You will need your entire strength for this."

Dravir turned to Ivan. He was doing much better. However he was still looking over his back occasionally to make sure Drakkon wasn't there. "Ivan, we need your help for this. You have to snap out of this or we will be overwhelmed." Ivan nodded slowly, then swallowed. "Alright" he muttered. "I am ready."

The four of them readied themselves. Ivan drew up his bow. Celandia activated Pozham Titania. Hersuls took to the air and Dravir drew *Gehenam*. Then they charged.

Ivan shot arrow after arrow at the Trolls and Orcs. Celandia turned Hellhounds into ash. Dravir slashed at Giants and Zombies, and Hersuls wrecked havoc from above. The sound of steel tearing into flesh echoed all over the wood.

The four fought hard. Sadly though, for every one they slashed, two more took their place. It was sheer hell. There were monsters to the left of them and monsters to their right. Ivan, Dravir and Celandia were backed up against each other, fighting frantically, while Hersuls dealt with the monsters from the air. "We are going to get overwhelmed." shouted Celandia.

Then like magic all the monsters disappeared and Grimoire spoke: "If you can't beat my monsters then you can't beat me. This is but a fraction of what I can do. Try and fight Atmos, you insects." This too was mocking and not out of concern. However the other Death Knight had different ideas. "No, if they couldn't even deal with your monsters then they won't be able to touch me." Atmos said, though he was still out of sight.

"Says who!" shouted Ivan. "I do," the airy voice came from different directions. "Don't underestimate my power. I am stronger than you will ever be. Even after death I will be greater than you. For I am a-" he stopped suddenly. An awkward silence followed. Dravir turned to Celandia, but was baffled by what he saw. There was a brief spell of triumph on Celandia's face, but was gone within the second. Atmos regained his composure and spoke "But if you do want to fight me I am more than obliged."

It was like an invisible pillow going a hundred miles per hour hit them. The four flew back, and tumbled. When they rose to their feet, it happened again, this time from behind them. This strange phenomenon occurred several times. Each time they were thrown back. By the end of it they had several bruises and cuts.

"Would you like to taste more of my power with the wind?" the Death Knight mocked. "The next time I strike, your bones will break."

Dravir started to back up towards Hersuls. "Come on, let's go, quickly." His voice was full of panic. "What?" both Celandia and Ivan turned around. "Don't you understand, we can't scratch any one of them! Staying here would be suicide!" "I agree." shouted Hersuls.

The Knaves quickly landed next to Dravir. Realizing what Dravir said was true, both Celandia and Ivan ran towards Hersuls. Dravir turned to face the Death Knights. "Aren't you going to stop us?" he asked, blade in hand. "No." Grimoire said. "You are far below us. Killing you would be beneath our dignity."

As they mounted Dravir spoke to the Death Knights. "Tell me just one thing. Shadow fist had four members, why don't you?" It was Atmos who answered; he materialized right next to Grimoire. "Yes, we do. Our fourth member is the most powerful member of the Death Knights other than Naxos and Croxeth.

Celandia gave out a gasp of horror. The names Croxeth and Naxos were unknown to Dravir. But judging by Celandia's reaction, he guessed that they were important people. "He is one of the heroes of the war with Altolen four years ago,"

"Rechin can kill Death Knight level warriors easily, but most of the time he's asleep." He said the last bit with a bit of shame.

"I hope you get a whooping from Croxeth for letting us go." Ivan said at that precise moment Hersuls flew into the air. "Croxeth won't whoop us, not while he's in that form." sneered Drakkon. "Rechin will make sure of that." With that the three figures melted into the shadows of the clearing once again.

CHAPTER 19

THE VALARI AND CRUXUS

"So," asked Dravir after three minutes of flying, "who are Croxeth and Naxos and why are they so scary?" "I've heard of them, they are the commander and second in command of the Death Knights. There are also two minor gods called Croxeth and Naxos. But that's probably a coincidence." said Ivan

"No, it's not." said Celandia, Dravir and Ivan gave her quizzical looks, even Hersuls slowed down. "My father has been working on a theory about the Death Knights and Orisis. You both know Orisis' position in the gods, right?" *'Please let this not be some kind of lecture about gods.'* Dravir prayed.

Neither Ivan nor Dravir nodded or said anything. "Fine then, Orisis or Ocathacaru is the head of nine powerful minor Gods, called Demipowers." Dravir wanted to hit himself. He had never been overly religious; he had never found it appealing. Now he was regretting not listening to his father's stories of the gods. He wanted to silence Celandia by saying that he knew what she was talking about.

Seeing Dravir's apparent confusion she explained further. "Each Demipower acts as an elite general, assassin or one man army, like the Doomknights. There's a reason there are nine Doomknights, one for each Demipower, it's a tribute to them."

"The Demipowers strictly serve only Skrall. My father believes that when Ocathacaru descended down to the world to become Orisis the other eight went with him. They took a place in his ranks, the Death Knights."

"Hold the wagon of crazy religious stuff on." said Dravir, "if they took places in his ranks, then why not become the Doomknights?" "Because" said Celandia slightly annoyed. "The Death Knights are a relatively older organization and have more mystiques surrounding them."

"The Demipowers are: Croxeth, Naxos, Rechin, Drakkon, Grimoire and Atmos. Each of them have large armies in the underworld and can strike effectively on short notice. We have to be very careful of what we do from here to keep ourselves alive."

"Wait," Ivan said "You said there were nine Demipowers." Celandia nodded. Ivan continued. "Well you have just told us the names of eight. Who is the last one?" Dravir raised his eyebrow and turned to Celandia. She smiled. "It's simple. One of the Demipowers, Vroth, returned to the Underworld. He now serves as an informant to Orisis." Ivan opened his mouth to say something, but he was defeated.

"Anyway what do you think?" she asked, turning to Dravir. "Honestly Celandia," said Dravir, "it really doesn't matter to us." Celandia scowled. "To Ivan maybe," she continued, "But for you, Dravir it matters. The Gods have taken sides and your side is heavily outnumbered." Dravir's eyes widened, "what do you mean?" it was clear from his voice that he was unsettled. "It means two sides have been formed, and if you're not careful, you could start a cross species war, with Gods."

Dravir started hyperventilating. "Who's on my side?" he asked badly trying to suppress the chaos and fear in his head "This is all an assumption. It could be give or take a couple gods: Morfos goddess of sleep and dreams is your mother, Krag lord of water, Bravec lord of the heavens, Yari goddess of nature, Ironia goddess of the forge and metals, Isnan lord of thieves, trickery, and luck, and Fujia, mistress of the winds."

Dravir slowly got his breathe under control. That wasn't so bad. They were all major gods who were known for their power. He spoke with a bit more confidence than before. "And who's on Orisis' side?" Celandia bit her lip and said "Skrall lord of the underworld, Lazex lord of war, Metistacia lord of time and space, Fuego lord of fire, Simain goddess of magic and wisdom, Croxeth, Naxos, Resis lord of vengeance, Drakkon, Atmos, Rechin and Grimoire.

"How do you know so much? I would have thought it to be a coincidence but this, this war that you're talking about actually seems to be folding around us." Ivan said. "I have a friend, back at the Ormis Baymis, who is a communicant of one of the minor gods; he tells me a lot of things." she said

And then as she finished she exclaimed "That's it, Resis is the last Demipower, number nine! Let's go straight away to the Ormis Baymis; my father's theory was correct!" Celandia was jubilant. However Ivan was not so enthusiastic. "That would be wonderful Celandia," he said with sarcasm. "Except for the fact that Edmund Shadoe is trying to resurrect two Knaves and that would lead to our immediate doom."

Celandia scowled at him. "I don't see you coming up with any great ideas then." Ivan snapped "Just because I haven't said anything doesn't mean I'm stupid!" Celandia snapped back "Really? You're giving us a good impression of it!" "WILL YOU TWO CUT IT OUT!!" roared Dravir. The argument ceased immediately and both participants looked at him.

"Look, Celandia, I'm sure that this theory is important and all, but we need to get to Edmund Shadoe and stop him from resurrecting the other two Knaves." Celandia looked like she was going to say something, but stopped herself.

There was a long uncomfortable silence after this, and just to break it Ivan said "Hersuls, how much longer till Shadoe castle . . . or whatever it is?"

"No need to wait," said Hersuls, his voice was strangely quiet. "It is right there." The three stared. They had been so wrapped around Celandia's God theory; that they hadn't realized that they arrived. Ahead, there was a massive black castle resting on a colossal mountain with the setting, red-orange sun right above it."

RESURRECTION ARC

CHAPTER 20

AMBUSH

"Hersuls take us down to the small town right there." said Celandia. Hersuls swooped down towards the small town careful to avoid detection; he finally found a small street to land in.

Dravir, Celandia and Ivan quickly dismounted. When Dravir had finished casting the invisible barrier that Duscuth had so many times used on Hersuls and themselves nine shadows appeared out of nowhere and surrounded them.

These shadows were not like the Death Knight ones, that if one saw behind a tree he or she could mistake it for a cloak. These shadows seemed much darker and older, if that was even possible. They were outlined with a pale yellow, the color of a bone.

Then the shadows dissolved and Dravir knew who they were standing before. Each man wore a black cloak with pale yellow trimmings and a hood, held a black staff with a human skull on it, and wore a silver skeleton mask. The Black Shadows had ambushed them. Strangely, like with Ishvala, there was a hand like cloud above three of them.

Then one yelled "Grazen, take to the skies, see if they are flying with a petty invisibility spell. Valhallus, search the ground around here. Vlas report to Shadoe. Noir, Muerte, you lot are here with me." Dravir saw three of the men return to shadow form and fly up, go towards the castle and fly down the street respectively.

Dravir turned towards Celandia whispered "Will we be able to take three down? There are four of us and we're not exactly weak." Celandia looked at him like he was crazy and whispered back. "Our chances with one of them would be rocky, two, with a good amount of luck; three will kill us." Dravir turned back to the necromancers. He had heard of them, but could they really be so powerful?

As if on cue, one of them, possibly Noir, lifted his staff somewhat higher and lowered it again with more speed and force. The sky immediately turned dark. In front of him a large circular pit appeared. Then a hand came out and held onto the ledge.

There was no flesh on that hand, just bone. This man was summoning the dead. More than a hand had emerged now. In fact two whole skeletal warriors had climbed out, and more were coming. Five minutes later there were twenty five fully armored undead warriors with swords, axes and war maces. It was truly a terrifying sight to behold.

"Nice one. That beats my record of twenty three in five minutes." said the one in the middle who had given orders. "This is not the time for records Constantine. We need to remove our target from this place." said the one who hadn't done anything so far. "So be it" said Constantine "I'll give them a little jolt." With that he did the same thing Noir did except after touching his staff down he murmured something.

What happened now struck terror into the hearts of Dravir, Ivan and Celandia. A pit, at least six times the size of Noir's was created. Dravir heard the flapping of wings. He closed his eyes, dreading what would happen when he opened them.

When he closed his eyes he saw Blaze, "What are you doing?" Pummel them! Don't give me crap like I'm not strong enough. Stop hiding and faced them like a man!" Blaze opened his mouth to say more but Dravir opened his eyes when he heard Ivan and Celandia's screams.

There, standing among the undead warriors and Black Shadows was a thirty foot tall undead dragon. Noir smirked, "We got them." A bolt of dark magic appeared right above his staff and he was about to hurl it right at the place Ivan was when someone threw a smoke screen down.

A figure emerged from behind them. He pointed to a door. "Get in, now!" No one said anything and all four of them ran to the door. And the mystery man closed the door behind them. Even behind the door they could hear Constantine's scream; "DAMN IT!! Where the hell did they go?"

Dravir turned around to see who had rescued them. It was a middle aged man wearing brown clothes. "Thank you for saving us." "No problem, the name's Enin Siser. I suppose you are Ivan" he said pointing to Dravir, "you are Dravir," pointing to Ivan "you are Celandia" he said finally getting one right. "And you are Hersuls." "Um no I'm Dravir." cut across Dravir. "How do you know our names?" Enin chuckled. "Everyone knows who you are. You think news of what you did to Ishavala Negundo wouldn't spread?"

"Here, I want to show you people something." Enin continued. Celandia suddenly stood up. "Dravir, Ivan, Hersuls, could I have a word?" Without waiting for an answer she pushed them to a corner away from Enin.

"What's this about, Celandia?" asked Ivan. "His name," whispered Celandia. "Celandia, this man just saved us from the Black Shadows, I don't give a damn what his name is." With that he walked back to Enin. Dravir was about to do the same but Celandia stopped him.

"You didn't happen to notice what his name was spelt backward, did you?" Dravir shook his head. "Why in Morfos' name would I notice that?" Celandia spoke with a shaking voice, "His name backwards is Resis Nine, and he is the last god who came with Ocathacaru." Dravir's eyes widened and he had only had one thought: to warn Ivan.

CHAPTER 21

THE DEAD AND THE TRAITOR

Hersuls, Dravir and Celandia quickly walked towards Ivan and Resis/Enin. When they sat down Resis/Enin got up and beckoned them to him. He walked to a door. "I have no idea what you people are doing here, but if you are trying to get into the dark mountain, there is a secret passageway right here leading to the wine cellar."

Before Dravir could intervene Ivan accepted the offer. Resis/Enin opened the door. From what Dravir saw it looked like a sewer without the water. Mossy bricks, dark and a *very* bad smell. Ivan gagged when he stepped in. "Does this place always smell like someone mutilated a rat?" complained Hersuls, as he stepped in.

Resis entered the tunnel without complaining or gagging. Dravir wondered whether the Demipower was immune to bad smells. "This way." muttered Resis. They walked in semi-darkness and silence for some time. Resis lead the group followed by Hersuls, Ivan, Celandia and Dravir. After what seemed like half an hour they saw a light up ahead.

They reached an oak door and Resis opened it. They were in the wine cellar. The room was made of wood. There were many cabinets that held wine. There was a barrel by the exit which was leaking something red, looking suspiciously like blood.

"There's the door!" said Ivan and then he rushed to it, his hand on the knob. "Are you mental!?!" cried Celandia "There could be guards or a patrol there." Dravir, Ivan and Hersuls looked at Resis who shrugged. "I have never done this before. I am relying on your expertise."

"All right," said Dravir "I'll open the door and if there is anyone one there you shoot them." Enin took a knife out of his belt, Celandia activated Pozham Titania, Hersuls took a breath, ready to blast fire and Dravir drew *Gehenam*. "Roar *Gehenam*" he whispered. The blade glowed red.

Dravir closed his hand on the door knob. A thousand thoughts ran through his head. What if this was a trap, what would happen to them if Edmund Shadoe himself was behind the door? What if they had to fight Resis? He and his friends had tackled lots of challenges, but fighting a God who wouldn't toy with them was impossible.

He turned the knob with his sweaty hand and slowly opened the door. He had only a few seconds to realize that it was a trap. A bolt a dark energy hit him in the chest with a great thud. Dravir was hurled back. Someone laughed. His vision was blurry but he was pretty sure he could see a few Black Shadows around the door.

"Well my Lord Resis," said the one on the extreme right. He was taller than Constantine had been, but not as muscled. "You have helped us and we expect you want payment." Resis looked at him for some time. "No payment needed Valhallus, currently. When I see the two brought back, and that the child of Morfos is dead then I will consider your debt settled."

Valhallus bowed. Resis erupted in shadows and disappeared. "Come, Lord Shadoe is waiting." The Black Shadows formed a circle around them. They walked. The castle was not as evil looking on the inside as it was on the outside. It was actually pleasant in a way.

They took a left turn down a hallway and the décor changed completely. The walls were black and draped in tapestries of painful scenes of death, and black cloaked figures summoning the dead. They led the company into a room with an elaborate circular diagram full of other shapes. A black version of the sun lay in its center.

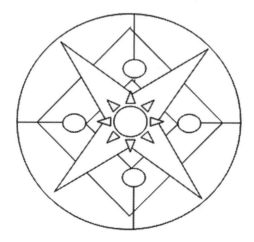

Edmund Shadoe stood in the black sun, smiling. "The guests have arrived. How nice, keep them by that corner. Make sure the Knaves doesn't escape, I want a family reunion." Then he turned back. "BLACK SHADOWS, TAKE YOUR PLACES!!" he roared.

The entire Black Shadows formed a tight ring around the circle. There were at least two dozen more than the ones that had come to ambush them. Shadoe stepped out of the sun and moved into the northern circle. "Constantine, Valhallus, Noir, take your positions. Three figures came out of the ring and took their positions in the three remaining circle. Shadoe snapped his fingers and two purple solid things gushing out goo appeared in the sun.

Dravir recognized two of the three. These three were obviously the higher ranking members of the Black Shadows. Shadoe began to chant something Dravir couldn't recognize. He shot a glance to Hersuls; his face was twisted with fear. Celandia and Ivan looked the same.

And Dravir realized one thing; the resurrection had started.

CHAPTER 22

LEGION 10, BRIGADE 4, DIVISION 6

They had to escape no matter what. *'A spell, any decent spell!'* thought Dravir. He constantly got distracted because of the chanting. He looked around and much to his surprise he saw a woman in light green robes. It seemed that the Black Shadows or Shadoe could not see her.

A huge fire erupted from the center of the circle. "Appease Hell!" a cackling voice said coming from nowhere. *"Devorabis omnes potentes mundo corrupto igne inferni!!"* chanted Shadoe; the Black Shadows immediately started chanting it.

He checked to see if Ivan, Hersuls or Celandia could see her, they could. Then the woman spoke. Her voice was full of power, but not hostility. "Hurry my child, my distraction can only grant you a limited amount of time. Especially with them around," She pointed to some of The Black Shadows. "Keres, servants of Ocathacaru, I will not be able to hide my presence for long."

"Facio cum his tenebris." The chanting was starting to speed up, the flame rising and dancing more furious than ever. The flame was starting to shape then a moment later it stopped.

"Um, anyone know what's going on? asked Ivan. Before Morfos opened here mouth to exclaim whatever strange occurrence was going on it became evident what was going on. The fire had somehow turned into lava and had now shot up in the form of an obelisk.

"I must act quickly, this will stun them for a couple of minutes, but the Keres will not be affected, I will engage them so you have a safe way to get out." This did not sound logical to Dravir. "But I can fight, I'll help you." said Dravir. "Do you want to die?" Morfos looked dead serious. "No." muttered Dravir.

Morfos pointed her hand towards the Black Shadows and issued a huge blast of light from it. Instantly the Keres attacked, their true forms showing; heavily muscled men with grey bodies, but their most strange feature was that they had the heads of wolfs.

At the same time the wall exploded and quite a few men charged in. They wore blue robes with chain mail under, and each wielded a crossbow or sword and two or three had staffs. "Rescue the Captain!" someone shouted. The Black Shadows were dazed by Morfos' blast of light, one even fell unconscious. Four men ran up to Celandia.

"Ma'am what are your orders?" one asked. Dravir looked at Celandia. Hersuls and Ivan had similar looks of bewilderment. "First get these ropes off us." Celandia said. Two of them immediately started chopping the black energy ropes.

"Now let's get the hell out of here, the enemy is starting to retaliate." Celandia commanded. One of the soldiers turned around and bellowed "FLEE, THE CAPTAIN HAS BEEN RESCUED!! MEET AT THE RENDVOUS!!!" With that the group of men ran out, this time with Hersuls, Dravir, Ivan and Celandia with them.

"Who are these people?" Hersuls asked Celandia. She smiled, then spoke "Legion 10, Brigade 4 Division 6, of the Ormis Baymis, my very own troops." She answered smiling. Then someone shouted something that shot chills down their backs.

Edmund Shadoe was laughing like a madman. "You may have won the battle, but we won the war, IT IS DONE!" Dravir turned around to see a skeletal wing come out from the ground where Shadoe stood.

"This is going to be a problem." muttered Dravir

HYORIN KATSURA ARC

CHAPTER 23

HYORIN KATSURA

Celandia men were moving fast. Dravir and Hersuls struggled to keep up. They reached a small plateau on the outskirts of the city, Celandia called a halt. Once the entire group was there, they started forming ranks. "When the troop form ranks, stand behind me to show you are friends and not foes." Celandia warned them while they were moving.

They did as Celandia had asked them. When the group had stopped stirring Celandia called out; "Casualty report!" Someone stepped forward from the front row "Ma'am only three injured, one has bit more injuries then the other two, but he'll be fixed up in no time. Frankly I'm astonished that they didn't do more damage, I thought we'd have more than ten d-" Celandia cut him off. "That will be enough Darren."

She turned to Dravir, Ivan and Hersuls and said "This is Darren my second in command." "Hello!" said Darren, he was monstrously tall, at least six feet five inches and had a huge broadsword strapped to his back. Despite his powerful and slightly overwhelming appearance he had a friendly glint in his eyes.

Celandia turned back to Darren, "How in the name of Krag did you find us." Darren grinned and answered "You'd be surprised to know what Zane does to keep his sister safe." After he said that four people started talking at the same time.

"Zane did what?" Celandia asked. Ivan coughed and said "Pardon?" Dravir asked "You have a brother?" And Hersuls said "Can you repeat that I didn't catch it." When the confusion and the exclaiming died down, Celandia turned toward Dravir Ivan and Hersuls. "Yes, I have a brother. But that is not important. We should focus on getting back to the Ormis Baymis quickly."

"No problem," said Darren "Our mages are finishing up a transport spell, we'll be there within the hour." This was good news and everyone was relieved. "Good." said Ivan. They walked towards the mages who were standing in a circle. One of them started to speak "Alright who's-" but he was cut off by a huge thud a good thirty feet away. Dust and dirt flew around. "Circle it!" Celandia shouted. The soldiers circled the area.

Suddenly a burst of energy flew out of the dust. It hit a mage. The thing continued to fire bursts of energy at them. Most of the mages had managed to put up defensive barriers, but some were slow. They were hit and fell. Eventually the thing stopped shooting, allowing the dust to settle.

When the dust cleared they saw the figure. It was Dravir's second time meeting him; Hyorin Katsura. He smiled. "Missed me?" Celandia, Dravir and Ivan drew their weapons. "I'm here to make sure you don't get an inflated head because you escaped Shadoe, bad news travels fast." Dravir pointed his sword at the Doomknight. "Why doesn't Shadoe come and get us then?' he challenged. Katsura laughed. "He is too busy flaunting his undead Knaves to Orisis." *That was fast.'* thought Dravir. It had been less than two hours since they had left the Dark Mountain

Katsura was holding the same stick that he held when they first set eyes on each other. He held it up. Dravir knew something bad was coming. "Dangai." The Doomknight whispered. A miniature red hurricane engulfed the cane. When it stopped it looked much different. He was holding a weapon like Dravir had never seen before. It was a halberd being held near the blade. On the regular grip side there was a bronze, wide and dented blade.

It was a ludicrous weapon for a ludicrous user. Katsura's fighting style was known to be unpredictable. It was said, that instead of mastering the traditional weapon forms, he created seventeen. He changed his form, and style at will.

Katsura swung his blade in Dravir's direction. Even though the blade hit nothing, an immensely fast wind hit them and threw them back. "*Sacer ingnis murum!*" shouted Dravir. The green fire shot forward and toward him, and then at the last second he was gone.

"*Bosen mannlich,*" Katsura was right behind them. "Much faster than shadow mist, it also lets me attack while performing it. I don't think it's that bad, considering I created it." He jumped back a couple feet and pointed the blade towards the group. "*Albtraum Null!*" A huge blast of red light hit Dravir straight in the chest and sent him flying.

The pain was overwhelming; he was bleeding all over and had probably broken a few bones, he blacked out for a couple seconds. When he opened his eyes it was like he was an onlooker, in his own body, he wasn't in control, but he was, at the same time. He looked at his limbs. They were black.

Then he laughed, it was mirthless, he did not know why he was laughing. "Yes, at last, you have succumbed to me." He rasped. It was not his voice. The voice belonged to Blaze.

This is what he meant when he said '*Well remember this, you may be able to perform demon magic now but I can't be suppressed now unlike Virard because I beat you!*' When he was too injured to continue, Blaze would. His inner spirit had now taken control of him.

He charged at Hyorin Katsura with speed more than his. He engaged Hyorin Katsura, who didn't look the least bit surprised with his transformation unlike his friends. If anything, the second Doomknight looked curious. As if he was observing some new animal.

The battle was completely one sided. Hyorin Katsura was not taking him seriously. He lazily flicked his sword around to deflect Dravir/Blaze's strikes and occasionally cutting Dravir/Blaze on his torso or legs. "I grow tired of this. In fluid movement he ran his blade through Dravir/Blaze's stomach. It caught them completely off guard.

Dravir/Blaze coughed out blood and fell to the ground. The last thing he heard before he hit the ground was his friend's screams and Hyorin Katsura say "Oops, I think I killed him . . ."

CHAPTER 24

WELCOME TO HELL!

Dravir awoke in a place he had never been before. It looked a lot like his inner soul when he had battled Virard except it was much, much larger. There was a huge gate ahead with a long queue of white translucent people behind it.

Dravir looked at himself. He was completely unchanged except for the fact that he was translucent and white. '*Well I'm dead.*' he thought. "That's where you wrong," a familiar voice said, behind. Dravir turned around.

It was Duscuth. Jubilation ran through him but it was short lived as he saw the look on Duscuth's face. "Duscuth . . . but how is this possible?" "Welcome to Hell. Relax Dravir, You will return to the land of the living with your full strength once more. But before that I must explain certain things."

"How can I trust you? You were the Sixth Doomknight. You served Orisis." there was resentment in Dravir's voice as he spoke. "The same reason that you trusted me when we were headed north. I was the only one you could trust, other than Hersuls." answered Duscuth.

"Fine, what is it that you want to tell me." asked Dravir. There still was a tiny bit of hostility in his voice. "I have only recently realized what will happen if you continue to be controlled by Blaze. You will slowly warp till you become an exact replica of him. And you're conscious will evaporate." Dravir would have to be an idiot not to know this was bad. He was not an idiot.

"Well that's going to be a problem. Got any way to destroy him?" asked Dravir. "Yes, but it's tricky and has to be timed correctly. You're going to need help from Skrall and Lazex."

"Wonderful." muttered Dravir. That possibility was ruled out. "I suggest that we enter the underworld for the Three Judges to pass judgment on us." said Duscuth. "After you . . ." They walked towards the bronze door and stood in the queue. After two hours it was their turn to enter.

The bronze doors opened and they walked through it. The floor was grey stone and there was no ceiling only black void above. There were three men sitting on a bench. They looked old, wise and they were the color of stone.

"Names" the man in the middle said. "Duscuth Ions and Dravir Xeres," the one on the right spoke. "Eh, interesting, I see you each have a good history and a bad one." said the one on the right. "But you didn't die did you sonny." said the one on the left pointing to Dravir.

"I um . . ." Dravir did not know how to respond. "He didn't," said Duscuth "Delanar's demonic soul theorem." Dravir didn't understand but it looked as if the old men did. "Very well," The middle one said. All three of them turned towards Dravir. "You didn't die, your Demon did." *'Finally, some good news.'* thought Dravir. "So Blaze is dead?" Dravir asked. "Not yet, once you die, he will die." "Oh well that simplifies things." muttered Dravir sarcastically.

"You don't know who we are, do you?" the one on the left asked. Dravir shook his head. "We are the Vilreal. We are the most powerful of the servants of Metistacia. We know how your fate will progress, and it is disturbing indeed."

"I don't suppose you couldn't tell me what is so disturbing about my fate right now." asked Dravir innocently. "No!" all three of the Vilreal said in unison. "It is against our ancient laws of time. We will not break it for the likes of you. We, however, can give you a little help."

"We will give you a choice; you can stay dead and go to The Hall of Pax. Or you can return to the living, and the next time you die, don't worry that won't be soon, you will have to except our ruling." This was an incredibly easy decision for Dravir.

"I chose to return to the land of the living." Dravir said. Duscuth smiled. "So you wish it so it will be; knowing your fate we must say that we hoped in vain. Good Bye!" With that, Dravir started floating up and disappeared into the darkness above.

CHAPTER 25

MORFOS' HELLFIRE PART 2

Dravir's broken form lay there with people huddled around it. The people were: Ivan, Hersuls, Celandia, Darren and some soldiers. The rest of the men had gotten clear. "I don't believe it . . ." Ivan said "I didn't think he would die so early in our quest." Tears followed from Celandia and Hersuls. Ivan did not cry. However everyone saw the pained expression on his face. Despite their rocky beginning, he had become fond of Dravir.

"Oi" said Dravir opening his eyes. Everyone jumped back. Celandia rubbed her eyes. "I'm hallucinating." She muttered. Dravir smiled. "I'm still here, I won't go that easily."

"How by Ironia are you still alive?" asked Hersuls. "Let's just say that creature took damage and not me." Everyone looked relieved. Celandia however, had some doubts. She sensed that Dravir was not telling the whole truth. She opened her mouth to voice her opinion, but was cut off by the worst thing imaginable.

"Well well well." someone said from behind them. It was Hyorin Katsura again. "You survived." He did not look the least bit caring. "I'll just kill you again." He smirked and brought his cane up and turned it into his bizarre blade. Ivan, Celandia and Hersuls backed up. The soldiers looked for cover.

Dravir, on the other hand, was brimming with confidence for some reason. "I don't think so!" he shouted. He stood up. There was a weird sensation in his gut. It was as if he had learnt something and wanted to try it. Dravir picked up *Gehenam*. "You have earned it my child, you may use it." A voice said in his head. It sounded like Morfos. Dravir charged, jumped up, an amazing eight feet, swung his sword and shouted "Morfos' Hellfire!!"

The blast of fire was more than Dravir had anticipated it was ten times bigger than *Sacer ingnis murum*. It took the form of a huge green bird made out of fire which consumed the Second Doomknight with a huge bang and a splatter of blood.

When the smoke cleared Hyorin Katsura was still standing, but with several cuts and small fires on him. He snarled and spat out "I'll be back!" With that he disappeared. Dravir collapsed. The attack had completely drained him. He turned to Celandia and said "Now, we head to the Ormis Baymis."

*　　*　　*

Unknown to the company that was rejoicing a Cassandra was hiding behind an elevation. She had heard every word they had spoken and knew where they were going. It was time to report to Shrukin she thought, the pieces were almost in play.

EPILOGUE

HEAVEN AND HELL

It was night. The cool air smacked Dravir's face stinging it. He was the only one still awake. The fire gradually got smaller and died. The only light in their small make shift camp was that of the stars.

His vision suddenly went black. When he looked again, there, ahead was a man. Dravir unsheathed *Gehenam*. The man turned around to face him. "Hello Xeres." The voice was like ice. Dravir's arm was shaking. He was in the presence of the Fear God.

Around him Drachen soldiers emerged from hiding spots. Dravir got up. He pointed his sword at Orisis. If it came down to it, he wasn't sure if he would be able to perform 'Morfos Hellfire' again. Orisis smiled, he was amused. "No I'm not here to kill you. I'm going to show you something. Something which will most probably influence everything you do after this." Orisis drawled.

"I want your word that you won't hurt Ivan, Celandia and Hersuls." Dravir said. He looked hard at Orisis and his men. Orisis met his gaze. "You have my word." said Orisis. The High King of Drachen turned around. "Disappear." He said. The soldiers turned and left. Orisis then turned back to Dravir. He snapped his fingers.

It was like Dravir was being sucked up a pipe at a hundred miles per hour. Finally when it stopped, he and Orisis were literally standing on a cloud. Orisis turned around, "Welcome to the Land of the Gods."

Five hundred feet above him there was a huge battle raging. "Those would be Rechin's troops fighting the soldiers of Pax, but you would know them as angels." Orisis explained. "A mere skirmish, it means nothing. These fools are constantly fighting."

"You see, I am helping you. This proves your friend's theory was right. The Demipowers are gaining power, and we're just waiting for you to do something stupid so that we have an excuse to declare war."

"I'm leaving you alone now. I have business to attend to. I will leave you to explore the heavens. Make the most of it, since you won't be coming back. My advice would be to go that way until you reach a city. Enter the city and meet your mother. Or, you could go that way," Orisis pointed in the opposite direction. "And literally 'go to hell'."

"I'm going to the city." Dravir said and turned around. He wanted to get away from Orisis. Something about conversing with Orisis, without any weapons drawn, unhinged him. Dravir began to walk. Orisis stopped him. "Xeres, despite what my Doomknights say; I don't hate you. I am amused by you. You see, the Drachen Empire is my way of killing time, I could easily take the entire continent but what fun would that be?"

"Sure." Dravir said and walked off.

He walked in the direction that Orisis had showed him. It seemed like ages till he got there. Occasionally he'd see a minor god running by, they'd stop tip their helmets and then continue running.

Then he saw it. The city that Orisis had talked about, the ordinary houses easily surpassed the greatest human palaces in beauty, except for the fact that the smallest were fifty feet tall.

There was a huge gate of gold in front of him which was at least two hundred feet tall. He nervously proceeded and knocked on the gate. It immediately opened. A man who was easily ten feet all came up to him. He looked at him with scrutiny "A mortal? We don't get a lot of your kind. What's your name?" "Dravir Xeres." The name seemed to shock the man. "Xeres eh? Right this way sir."

He followed the man through the city until they got to a large purple palace. "Your mum's expecting you." He man said before leaving. Dravir walked up the steps which had seemed to magically change to fit his size.

When he reached the top he saw Morfos talking with a man. She turned and saw him. "Lord Rehk can you leave us? I wish to speak with my son in private." Lord Rehk smiled, as if there was something funny. "Very well, I understand." The man said and bowed. As he walked out he winked at Dravir.

Morfos walked up to him and did the last thing Dravir expected her to do. She slapped him. "Why did you do that?" he asked, rubbing his cheek. "How could you believe that Orisis would not be hostile? You are not supposed to go to places with strangers." The Goddess of sleep shouted.

Dravir found the last statement a little odd. "Technically Orisis isn't a stranger." he said. "Oh yes, he's your demented, evil cousin who wants to kill you because you might ruin his little empire." Morfos replied sarcastically.

"Evil I can stomach, but demented, I think your being a little unfair." Someone said from behind them. Morfos' nostrils flared. "Be gone from here Ocathacaru, you live here no longer!" Morfos shouted. Dravir heard a sigh and then a loud crack.

"So who was that man you were talking to?" asked Dravir. "Lord Rehk, he's the God of laws and one of our top generals." Morfos answered. "So it is true that the Gods are going to war?" Dravir asked. "That depends on whether you do something stupid or not." She replied tartly.

"Everyone says if I do something stupid, but no one tells me what they mean, I need an explanation. How else am I going to stop myself from doing anything stupid?" said Dravir, who was very irritated by all the vague answers he got.

"Don't do anything provocative. Especially when dealing with Lazex and Skrall. Those fools will take the slightest offense to a catastrophic level." Morfos replied. Dravir was confused and irritated. "Please clarify something for me, mother. Am I supposed to dethrone Orisis or not? Killing Orisis' physical body; might be provocative."

Morfos muttered something. Dravir had an idea of what she was saying. He caught words like 'insolent', 'shameless' and 'ridiculous'. She looked up at him. "You are being sanctioned. You are free to depose Orisis. Just make sure you don't burn any temples." Dravir sighed. "Well, that's fine. I don't plan on doing that."

Morfos smiled. "I have faith in you." Her face then returned to its normal frown. "You should go. Your friends will awake in mere hours."

"I want to speak with Orisis one more time." Dravir requested. Morfos sighed "As you wish." "FEAR GOD" she shouted "YOUR PRESENCE IS REQUIRED!!!!"

Orisis materialized in front of them. "Yes." He said sourly. "I wish to speak with you." said Dravir. "Let us talk" replied Orisis "Yes, but in private, mother will you leave us?" "Very well." said Morfos

"You told me that you could strike me down at any time you wished, but I understand something now." Dravir said, arrogantly "if you did it would guarantee this war, which would take its toll on you. Basically; you can't kill me." Dravir continued cockily, but he almost immediately took it back. Orisis' eyes were a cold, dark abyss. "Shall I show your insolence something?" asked Orisis mockingly.

He didn't wait for a reply, it was the some sucking sensation that Dravir had felt earlier only this time he was going downward.

When it finally finished Dravir opened his eyes. He could not describe his surroundings; they were too terrible to explain, figures of darkness and evil combined with fire and brimstone were all over the place and one could hear the cries of tortured souls in the distance. "Welcome to hell." said Orisis. "Wait this place can't be hell; I've been to hell before. Dravir said. He was now visibly shaking with fatigue and breathing a lot faster than normal. He was succumbing to the depths of hell.

"I assume you know what layers are?" asked Orisis. "Yes." croaked Dravir. He was almost on his knees and gasping for breath, unable to comprehend Orisis' ability to be indifferent in their current situation.

Orisis sighed "You're a half god aren't you, that's why you've lasted so long." He paused for a second then continued "I suppose I have to save you now, what a twist to reality."

He tapped Dravir on his chest, around the lungs and muttered something, immediately pure air rushed into his lungs and his colossal fatigue disappeared. Dravir breathed in. "Follow me." said Orisis coldly.

They walked in an unnamed direction. The strange part about this was the fact that there was nothing above or below him. He was suspended in midair. Dravir had long lost his sense of time so he did not know how long they walked.

At long last they come to a gate. It was shaped like a human skull with the doors in the mouth. The gate was terrible to behold. It was made of rusted bronze and had various scenes of torture and pain engraved which were terribly unsettling to Dravir.

Orisis knocked on it three times and it opened releasing a thick cloud of dust, Dravir shielded his face to stop the dust from getting in his mouth and eyes.

"Behold the ancient ones." In the room, which was just made up of a few walls there were three men other then himself and Orisis. "Boys will you introduce yourselves to my *special* friend.

The first one turned around. He had a crazy bloodlust-like look in his face, like Hyorin Katsura on a sugar rushed killing spree, "Sanguis." He said. Dravir could tell just by his voice that this creature was insane and obsessed with killing. "Fear god version one." He continued.

Despite his insane expression his eyes were vacant and he gave out the impression of great stupidity. He had dark drown skin that looked withered and worn.

"He was the Fear god a few thousand years ago, but he was replaced because he went a little sideways in the intelligence department." said Orisis. Conveniently Sanguis started licking his toes. "Yummy bears." he growled. Orisis looked at Dravir. "I can see that." said Dravir taken aback.

The second man turned around, he was seemingly a bit normal except for two things. He had four thin black, spider legs coming out of his back and he had red fangs.

"Valthor, he is fear god version two." He had a hair of spiky orange hair and his pupils were red. "He was the fear god after Sanguis; he represented primal fear, when men were hunted and hunters. He was replaced when men learned to defend themselves properly."

The third person was no closer to the norm. As he turned around he could feel the fear eating him alive, this one was easily more powerful than the previous two, combined, perhaps even more than Orisis.

The first thing that Dravir realized about him was that he was huge at least eight feet tall. He had long, rough, uneven white hair coming down to his waist, heartless icy eyes and three horizontal scars on his nose as well as one going through the left part of his lip. He had on a jet black Ō-yoroi[1] and had a knee length sleeveless blood stained, silver haori[2].

On his left side there were two sheaths with katanas in them. But his most fearsome weapon was his irregular spear. Dravir suspected that the shaft was actually an exceptionally thin lance, as the shaft's shape was as such. If it was a lance a long curving blade was hooked onto the regular griping part.

But the man's most strange feature was that he had two long velvet-like black wings coming out of his back. "My name is Futaken Lishavas. I was replaced because I was too unpredictable, uncontrollable, if you may." Lishavas smirked.

"You see," said Orisis "I don't have to strike you down, Sanguis will blindly obey me if I ask him, and who will believe him when he tells the gods that I told him to, when I am humbly governing a mortal Empire."

---

[1] A Ō-yoroi is the name of a Samurai armor that came out in the late Heian period
[2] A Haori is a kimono-like jacket, which adds style and rank/formality to any piece of clothing

"Yes, but we'll know won't we." said Valthor. Orisis looked at him angrily. "It would be better for your health if you didn't say anything though." Orisis said his fist suddenly setting itself on fire.

Valthor gulped and shrank back. Orisis turned back to Dravir "It's time for you to leave; I have some *business* with my brothers that I have to take care of."

For the third time that night Dravir had that same sucking sensation as he shot upward back to the camp. *'This is a tricky situation I'm in. If what Orisis said was true he could kill me at any time he wished. I need to get stronger, I need help, and more power.'* Dravir thought to himself before he sank back down for at least twenty minutes of sleep.

*   *   *

Unknown to Dravir, when Orisis left Hell he did not seal the gate. At first the three ex gods did not realize this but Futaken Lishavas stared at the gate unable to put his finger on what was different.

The elder fear god was not mentally deficient like Sanguis, in fourteen minutes to realize that the gate was not sealed. Quietly he unsheathed one of his katanas. "It has a pleasure serving with you." He said loud enough for both his companions to hear him. They spun around. "*Kame-shini no kaze!*" Lishavas shouted. Both ex gods fell back dead. Futaken smiled and sheathed his sword. Now the time was ripe to extract his revenge on the one who had broken him.

The fear god was loose.